ONCE UPON A

DREAM

Steena Holmes

ONCE UPON A DREAM

Steena Holmes

ISBN: 1-894928-64-4

Printed by Word Alive Press

WORD ALIVE PRESS

Acknowledgements

What an incredible dream to come true! This book is living proof that God hears all the hidden dreams in our hearts. I can imagine Him smiling down at me, rubbing His hands together in expectation, just waiting to see my reaction the moment I realized my dream has come true!

There are so many wonderful friends that I need to thank for helping me:

J.H. - Jen, you were always there to answer all my desperate pleas of help.

K.H. - girl, I always knew when you hit the romantic spots. Thank you for believing in the romance.

C.M. - Rich Carradine was created for you.

Creative Grace Gals - your encouragement and kick in the pants were what I needed so many times.

Jarrett, the love of my life - you believed in this dream and encouraged me to run with it. I am indeed blessed to be loved by you.

Finally, to all those at Word Alive who gave me the opportunity to see this dream become reality - Caroline, I still remember the shock when you called me to tell me I won the contest! All I have been able to say since then is, "Wow God!"

Thanks again!

Steena

Prelude

THE SMELL OF HAZELNUT COFFEE lingers in the air. What a wonderfully delicious aroma to wake up to. I need to program my coffee maker to do this every morning. Imagine how productive I could be if the coffee was already made before I woke up! Well, at least I could try to imagine. A morning person I am not—coffee or no coffee.

My bed is so warm, almost as if I'm cocooned in warmth. Wouldn't it be nice to stay in bed all day, wearing silky lingerie, and the warmth all around me, and coffee right beside me, so all I have to do is stick one hand out of the blanket and bring the coffee to my lips? What a treat that would be!

I've never worn silky lingerie all day before, let alone one night... wait a minute... I've never worn any type of lingerie before. Where did I get this? Perhaps I need to drink the whole pot of coffee before my brain starts to work properly. Hmmm, the taste. Absolutely perfect. What a sweetie to have brought me this... a sweetie? I don't have a sweetie. In fact, why is there coffee beside me? I don't have a machine that makes coffee on its own. Who made this coffee? And why is my bed warm? I must still be asleep. In fact, I have to still be dreaming, because in my dream this would all make sense. Of course, in my dream my life is perfect. But then, isn't it always that way?

Ok, let's not panic. Slowly slide back down underneath the covers, close your eyes and go back to your dream. It was so perfect. I had just gotten married, now why I didn't dream about the actual wedding is beyond me, but I know I was married. Rather, I was dreaming of what happened after the wedding. The love of my life, a quiet evening of romance. Falling asleep in his arms. Waking up to a gentle kiss, and hearing footsteps go into the kitchen. A dream of contentment, peace and love. If I could only go back to that dream... but the smell is still there. Hazelnut coffee. And I'm still wearing something silky.

I peek my head above the covers and see clothes that are definitely not mine. Ok, deep breathes. In, out, in, out... deep breaths. Breathe, breath. This can't be happening. It has to be a mistake. What happened last night? I lift my left hand out of the covers and see a ring. A ring! WHAT! Oh my gosh, breathe, breathe. This breathing thing is not working. Where is my paper bag?! I'm starting to panic for real now. Are those footsteps I hear? Oh my... they are. I duck down underneath the covers and with eyes closed tightly I try to will myself to sleep. This has to be a dream. I am dreaming. I just know I am.

"Good morning love, time to wake up sleepy head."

It's his voice. Oh my. Please God, let me be dreaming! Ok, take a breath, and be bold. I peek out the corner of the covers and see him standing there. In MY doorway. This cannot be happening. Absolute perfection is standing in my bedroom, and he's holding a cup of coffee in one hand, and a chocolate croissant in the other. Oh my. OH MY! I decide to be bold. After all, this is my bed, my bedroom and my house. I hold the covers to my chin and muffle, "Am I dreaming?"

Chocolate is the perfect
remedy for chasing away
those rainy day blues.

Chapter 1

"HELLO DARLING! ANYBODY HOME?" calls out a shrilly voice.

Startled, I half fall off my couch. With my body half on my couch, and half on the floor, I realize that this is not the voice in my dream. The one in my dream was male, husky and full of laughter. This voice is shrilly, loud and definitely female.

"Hellllooo? Wynne? Where are you?" that voice beckons once again.

"Ugh, in here Susan," I call out—half hoping that when she sees me, she'll immediately come rescue me, instead of giving me the reaction that I know is about to come.

As she begins to place her overloaded bag on the floor, Susan peeks around the doorway and immediately drops her bag in a burst of laughter.

"What are you doing?" she manages to get out. "You're supposed to be laying on your couch resting, not doing gymnastics! Although," she muses, "that position does look kind of interesting!" she squats on the floor, tilting her head so that she can get a better view of my face.

"Oh, just help me up, will you? Stop laughing at me! I'll have you know I was sleeping before you barged into my home!" I tried to sound quite indignant.

I managed to right myself off the floor, albeit with a little bit of grunting and stretching of body parts that I didn't know I had, but I placed myself back on the couch. I covered myself back up with my blanket and tried to make the most pathetic looking face I could manage.

"I'll have you know, I didn't barge! I was knocking but no one answered. Knowing you are not feeling well, I brought over some treats to take care of you with." Susan lifts up her overflowing bag. "Just lay back down, go back to sleep, and I'll wake you when everything is ready," she calls over her shoulder as she meanders into my kitchen.

"Go back to sleep? If only I could. You startled me so much that I'm wide-awake. How come you're here? How did you know I was home today and not at work?" I asked her. I could probably answer that without using much brainpower, but at the moment any type of brainpower usage is causing my brain to hurt. Since I figured it would be kind of rude to fall asleep with someone in my home, that same someone being a person who is kind enough to come and take care of me, I decided to snuggle deeper into my comfy soft couch with my warm blanket and prepared myself to be pampered!

Susan Manning, a gourmet chef who just happens to be one of my closest friends and ex-roommate, is the one pampering me. She is tall and elegant, and the phrase "a moment on the lips, means a lifetime on the hips" definitely does not apply to her. You would never know that she taste tests everything she creates. She did the one feat all single women dream of—she caught and captured her white knight. She also did the unmentionable and betrayed me by getting married! So now I live alone in my spacious home, feeling sorry for myself each and every night.

"You forget that I'm married to your business partner. He called me up this morning to inform me just how pathetic you sounded when you called. I'm here to rescue you, and to keep you from contaminating the store. Call me your personal pampering guardian!" she proclaims as she takes a bow from her waist.

"I'm here to make sure you don't go into the store today," she continues to explain while bringing me a cup of tea. Hmmm, hot honey and lemon.

"Please tell me you're also here to make me your famous chicken noodle soup!" I begged as I took in the soothing aroma of the tea. This will definitely help to relieve my sinuses.

You know when you are feeling blah; the only thing to do is console yourself with comfort food. If I weren't so sick, I would have some type of chocolate to enjoy. But being how I have a head cold, the only thing to cheer me up is a warm blanket, some hot tea, and Susan's ultimate chicken noodle soup. I don't know what she puts in the pot, but it's absolutely delicious!

"Of course I am. What type of friend would I be if I left you here in misery without my soup?" bragging just slightly, Susan commented. "Now just relax. Dream of chocolate or some handsome fellow bringing you chocolate! I'll wake you when the soup is done."

Feeling satisfied, and a bit drowsy at the same time, I murmur, "You're a sweetie. Even if you did leave me to get married, you're still a sweetie!"

As I drift off to sleep, I can hear a chuckling in the background.

All right, I'll admit it. So I might have some issues with being single. Can you really blame me? My number one issue mainly consists of the fact that all my friends seem to desert me for some guy. And yes, I might feel sorry for myself for being single. But, and this is my answer to everything, God and chocolate can solve all my problems! If you haven't been able to tell so far, there are two passions in my life, chocolate being one of them! And if you catch me at the right time, sometimes I'll even admit it's the first major passion in my life. God is my other passion. I realized early in life that the only way I can remain single and sane at the same time is to keep my focus on Him. Which also brings up one major issue that I have. Being single. This is definitely not my calling, but rather my un-chosen way of life. Not to say that I haven't had the opportunity to walk down the other path called marriage. Cause I did. That is my one upstanding moment as a single. I had that most sought after opportunity by all females to walk down the rose-layered aisle, and I chose to not take it. I realized that my desire to be married to the right guy outweighed my desire to no longer be single. This being said though, that decision left me with the necessity of having to buy a house and to be the primary caretaker of myself when I get sick.

After being spoilt silly by Susan and then taking a long hot bath, I cuddle up in my big lonely bed and drift off to sleep. I'm having the most wonderful dream ever. I am in a ballroom that is decorated to perfection. There is soft music being played by an orchestra in the far corner. Candles are the only light source in the room. There are the smells of fresh cut flowers surrounding me, filling all my senses. Waiters in black tuxedos are walking through the throng of people offering glasses of sparkling apple juice (hey, it's my dream, and I don't drink). I know that there are people all around me, but they all appear a blur. For in that moment, I realize that I am dancing in the arms of a very strong, handsome man. The man of my dreams. He's wearing a black tux, and has a cologne on that I know will haunt me as a smell that will always be just beyond my reach. He's the man of my dreams. Always the same one. I never look into his face, yet I know him deep in my heart. We're dancing. I'm wearing a gorgeous Vera Wang gown (again, it's my dream!) and I feel it sweeping as we move across the floor. In graceful steps, swaying to the beautiful music, I feel secure, wanted and loved. It's the perfect night. I begin to turn my head to look into his eyes. I've decided to tell him how I feel. As my head begins to turn, I... THUMP!

I fall off my bed.

What a way to end a romantic dream!

It's amazing how much pain one feels from falling from their bed while they're sleeping. Not only does my head hurt from hitting my night stand, but my shoulder is twisted under me in a way that is not comfortable, my flannel nightgown is so twisted around my legs that I can't move them if I tried, and I think I landed on my nose. With my free hand (the one that's not twisted under me) I feel my nose and realize I'm bleeding. Just great! My first nosebleed ever, and it's from falling out of bed! And on my hand braided bed rug for that matter! This is not turning out to be a great day.

Somehow I manage to get myself untwisted just as the phone rings. With a disgruntled tone that is somewhat muffled by the Kleenex that I have stuck up my nose, I answer.

"Well, good morning to you, too, Sunshine! Don't tell me I just woke you up. It's already 8 AM. You're not sounding that great, maybe you should get right back into bed and stay home again. Matt and Lily can handle the store for another day," answered Susan in that too-early-in-the-morning bubbly sort of voice.

"My nothe ith bleeding. Call you bach," was my reply while running to the bathroom. Nothing I hate more than a mess to clean up off my floors. I hang up without hearing her reply and take a good look at myself in the mirror. My head is tilted up to stop the bleeding, my hair is in a wild disarray, and I have drool lines down the one side of my mouth. Quite attractive, if I do say so myself. It's on mornings like this that I'm glad I'm still single. I still can't believe that I fell out of bed. The memory of that dream still lingers, and I can still feel strong arms around me as we are dancing to soft music. If only reality could be like my dreams, I would be happy and satisfied.

I know, I know, give thanks in all things. Am I actually to take that scripture literally? I have to be thankful that the only romance in my life comes by my dreams, that falling out of bed appears to be my way of life, and no one is around to help me when my nose bleeds? Count it all joy. When I think of that verse, I see myself fluttering around like a little cherub angel, wings sprouting from my back, dancing around on little white fluffy clouds, singing, "Joy, joy, count it all Joy." I don't think so. What does that mean anyways? If a single man or woman could explain that to me—how they have applied it to their life as a single person and actually had it work—then I might listen. But when all my married friends give me that little smile and tell me to count it all joy... my only thought is to flick their ear and see if they can count that as joy!

Being cleaned up and looking halfway presentable, I call Susan back.

"Morning Sue. Was there an honest to goodness reason for calling me so early in the morning?" was my greeting even before she could say hello.

"Umm, I think you are wanting Susan," it was Matt who answered. "I'll let her try to talk you out of this mood before you come into the store today," he replied before I heard the phone drop and his voice say in the background, "I don't know what you did, but Wynne doesn't sound too happy. Good luck."

"Wynne. What did Matt do to deserve your morning grumpiness? Don't tell me you didn't have a good sleep? Did you fix your nose? I couldn't quite grasp what you were saying before you hung up so quickly!" Susan tried to unsuccessfully admonish me.

"Humph. My morning grumpiness! Look who's talking! I'll have you know I was having a perfectly romantic dream before you called. I fell out of bed this morning and my nose started to bleed. No, don't laugh! It was a perfectly good dream too! I almost saw his face this time!"

Susan knows all about my dreams. I've been having these for the past year or so. At first I found it very exciting... dreaming about a man I thought I knew, but never seeing his face. Now it's getting down right frustrating! If this is God's way of preparing me for a new love life, He has a funny way of doing it.

"You almost saw his face? Wow. Go back to bed then and start dreaming again! I still say that it's Rich you're dreaming of," Susan tells me.

"Sue, it can't be Richard. We've already gone through with this. He's married. I'm sure he has two kids and a dog by now. I can't be dreaming of him, that would just be wrong! He's been out of my life for too long for me to start thinking of him again. Nope, this has to be someone else. Someone who can take his place in my heart," I tell Susan. So maybe I'm in denial. But to agree with her would be detrimental to my heart.

"You don't know he's married Wynne. You just think he is," Susan tells me in a patronizing tone of voice. "You heard he was getting married, but maybe, and this could be true, he didn't actually get married. Did you ever think it could be like you? He probably thinks you're married as well. I don't understand why you don't try to find him and find out," she tells me in her exasperated tone. We've had this discussion many times.

"Because Sue, you don't just start searching for someone out of the blue! What if I do find him. Do I call him up? What if his wife answers, or girlfriend—how do I explain to them or to him the reason for me calling? No. I don't think so." I tell her with a note of finality in my voice.

"Alright, you live in your dream world. The reason I called is to tell you I'm sending a surprise over with Matt this morning. This is the official phone call to tell you to keep your hands off! I want you to have complete deniability, at least for the first customer. You'll need to add your own little personal touch to the boxes, but do not look inside! Now, I gotta run, before Matt leaves without this stuff. Talk to you later," and she quickly hangs up.

That was so not fair! Knowing her, she has made up something that tastes delicious! She always does this to me. She will make something for the store, but won't let me in on the secret. I always have to wait until someone will tell me what it is. Once in a while I'll take a peek, but I've experienced her wrath too often to do that anymore. She doesn't play fair! And she knows it.

In anticipation of what I will find when I get to the store, I quickly finish getting ready. I need to remember to take the muffins that I took out of the freezer last night and placed in the fridge to defrost. I always find myself excited to go into my store. A new day awaits, and it's been a few days since I have been there. I trust Matt to keep it running smoothly, but he doesn't quite have that woman's touch, so something is always lacking if I've been away for longer than a day.

My phone rings as I head out the door. My arms are full of muffins, so I just let the answering machine take it. If it's important enough, everyone knows to call me at work.

Chocolate is the one great
passion of life that is
ALWAYS there.

Chapter 2

CHOCOLATE BLESSINGS. My great passion. As I enter the door with the jingle of bells, I take a deep breath and sigh. The smell of chocolate and flowers is amazing. I co-own this oasis with Matthew Manning, my ex-roommate Susan's new husband. I have the love for chocolate and he has all the business savvy, and together we make a great team, if I do say so myself. Having only been in business for two years, we are already experiencing more growth than I dreamed of. With that growth comes long hours though. Especially this time of the year. Christmas. The number one gift preferred. Who in their right minds would actually turn down chocolate? And not just ordinary chocolate! We even offer delicious sugar free chocolate! Chocolate Blessings has everything you can think of to help showcase the gift of chocolate to the finest degree. Not only do we offer chocolate, but we also help our local community by taking in one of a kind gift items that are made locally. Our hand selected gift basket ideas are a hot seller right now. Who knew that I would be able to turn a love for chocolate into a profitable career!

Right now the sound of Christmas music is heard throughout the store. Fresh bouquets of flowers, which are bought from a florist next door, can be found throughout the store. We offer a fresh cut rose free with every order—a little touch that I have found the female customer just loves. Our showcase of chocolate is fully stocked, shelves are lined with gourmet boxes of chocolate, and I even see a few new gift ideas out. Mental note to self: check out new gift ideas and find more!

Lily, our front clerk, greets me warmly. "Wynne, it's so good to see you! It's been a long three days without you here. How are you feeling? You definitely look better! Oh, I have so much to tell you!"

Lily, if you can't already tell, is a bubbly young adult. In her young adults group at church, she has been classified as the bubbly blond greeter. As soon as someone walks into our church, the only way it is possible that they would not be immediately greeted with her bubbly smile and laughter is if she is currently greeting another new person to walk into our church. Having these characteristics, I found it to be a blessing when she agreed to come work for me here. She is the perfect person to have at the front counter. If you have no idea what to buy as a gift, she will always make sure that you don't leave empty handed!

"Well hello, Miss Lily! I've missed being here. But I'm back in action. How are you doing? Oh, is there any hot apple cider ready? My whole focus for the morning was to get in here and have a cup! Here, can you put these muffins in the display for me?" I asked her as I passed the container of muffins over the counter to her.

A few months ago I decided to section off a small corner with some garden tables and chairs. I thought it would be a wonderful place to sit and chat while enjoying a treat. So we offer gourmet hot chocolate, flavored coffee and tea, and with the season upon us, warm apple cider. The idea has been a hit, and it's very rare that you won't find the tables full of laughter. If you listen closely, you can even hear those satisfied sighs of delight once they breathe in the aroma of their hot beverage and taste their chocolate treat!

"I just put on a fresh pot! That's been a hot commodity the past few days. Oh, and there was a message from Pastor Joy. If you were feeling up to it, they would still like to meet this morning here for coffee. I told her you would call her right away!"

Every Thursday morning a group of ladies from our local church meet here for coffee. We are called the Latte Ladies. There are five of us who meet for coffee, chocolate and prayer. These ladies have been my morning cup of sanity many times. As I am the youngest of the bunch, I get to be mothered and mentored by four older women on a regular basis. I have to admit that I love it! It was my Latte Ladies who gave me the push to create Chocolate Blessings. And it was this group of special ladies who gave me the courage to not walk down the aisle of doom. With that in mind... I had better give Pastor Joy a call.

As I grab a cup of warm apple cider, the bell above the door jingles. In walks Matthew, carrying brightly wrapped boxes.

"Well good morning, Sunshine." He greets me using his nickname for me. "Good to see my wife's pampering did the job! I was beginning to get worried that I would have to place those tiny little nuisances you call ribbons and bows on these boxes." Matthew has a brilliant mind, one that is constantly running. The only thing is, along with that brilliant mind, he's also very logical and practical. While he agrees that the little things in our store help to sell our product, trying to figure out just what those little things are is beyond his comprehension.

"Here, let me help you with those. I was just about to head back into the office anyways." I grab a few of the boxes while trying to juggle my dripping cup of cider. I have specific instructions that I'm not allowed to peak inside, but a delicious aroma is escaping one of the boxes I am holding, and I'm finding myself sorely tempted to go against those orders!

"Hmm, what's inside? Is this what Susan told me about this morning? I don't recall her telling me what she made though. Care to share? Hmm, why don't I just peek instead?" I suggested. I'm hoping that Susan didn't tell him I'm not allowed to peek. I dislike surprises with a passion, especially if I know about them. Just the knowledge that there is something, but I'm not allowed to know what that something is, gets to me. I'm just the type of person who needs to know. Especially when it comes to chocolate! Keeping chocolate a secret just is not fair. I feel like a little kid in a candy store, then I find myself actually giggling out loud, cause in reality, I actually am a big kid in a chocolate store!

"Susan made these, and they are a surprise. She specifically told me to tell you hands off! You're allowed to help wrap them all pretty like, but then that's it. They are that surprise gift we talked about last month," Matt explained while trying to maneuver around all the displays, the front counter and then around the office door in the back.

Last month Matthew and I were trying to think of creative ways to attract more gift buying. I thought of a surprise gift that comes decorated in an elegant box with ribbon and bows. We would either sell it separately or include it in a gift basket.

He loved the idea, anything to generate more income, and decided to ask Susan if she would mind creating a special holiday chocolate for this in mind. I'm assuming that she said yes, for the evidence is in these boxes. Considering chocolate is involved, I'll have to wait until he is out of the office before I open a box. As if I could really keep my 'hands off' as I was told to do!

As we walked into our tiny office, the phone was ringing. Answering it I heard, "Put on fresh coffee cause we're coming over!" giggles, and then a click. I chuckle. That has to be the Latte Ladies! Probably Joan. She's quite the character! Always has a smile on her face, and you just can't help but to smile when you see her! I can imagine that today she will be wearing some type of Christmas earrings that dangle, light up or sing a song. She will probably be wearing her Christmas jacket and will have a song in her head that she will be humming out loud.

"Who was that?" asked Matt. Then he looks at the calendar, sees the big coffee mug stickers that are placed on every Thursday, and said, "Let me guess, your coffee ladies! Hey, get them to buy a box, and then you can see what is in them!" What a nice guy, offering me a way out of having to willfully disobey one of Susan's many orders!

"I think I might just do that... if you hurry and hand me the ribbons and bows!"

Have I mentioned yet just how much I love my "Latte Ladies" group? It's with this group of ladies that I can be real. As I'm the youngest, they love to mother me, and I love to be mothered. I always know that with this group, I am held up in prayer, and any advice I am given will be based on the Word of God. They are quirky, serious, fun and safe.

I walk out of my office with my arms full of these mystery boxes only to be greeted by the doorbell jingling and laughter filling the store. My Latte Ladies have arrived!

"Hmmm, something smells good!"

"Oh, she put apple cider on! She must love us."

"Chocolate and coffee—the best of friends"

"Oh, what do you have in those boxes? I want one!" Are the greetings that begin from the moment they enter the store. It's when I hear comments like those that I know I'm in my element.

As I juggle the boxes in my hand, the ladies come over to help me arrange them on the shelves. I find my mouth beginning to water with the knowledge that soon I'll be able to find out what type of creation Susan made, for I know each of the ladies will take one for themselves.

"Oh, what do we have here? Hmmm, it smells delicious! Oh, and it's a secret! Wynne, where do you come up with the ideas! I'm gonna have to grab one of these. Tracey, you take one too; you need to put some weight on that body of yours. Judy, won't these be perfect gifts for our Secret Sister's group? Oh, and we must add a few of these to the Christmas baskets. Pastor Joy, you know you can't turn up chocolate! Wynne, why do you always seem to be placing new product out when we arrive in the store! Shame on you, as if we could ever deny ourselves the pleasure of your sweets!" Joan Hollingway exclaims in her rapid fashion of speech. Meet Joan, the one lady in our group who has a habit of talking rather quickly when she gets excited. And if you haven't already figured it out, chocolate in any form gets her excited.

As each lady grabs her box, favorite treat and coffee we head over to the café section of the store. I made sure that I created this space with coziness in mind. It has the look of an outdoor café, but with the warmth of homemade coziness. Cushions on each seat, handmade tablecloths and antique furniture to grace this little corner. Since this is an area where you sit and chat, I have placed many of my handmade items for sale in this area. From plaques, to stitchery designs, tattered pillows and quilts. Handmade dolls, candles, sheep of all sorts, quilts and fabric. So many wonderful ladies create these products, and it's continually being updated with new product on a weekly basis. I firmly believe in showcasing these items. I know personally how much love and care goes into every single stitch and design. When Matt and I first opened Chocolate Blessings, we began with consignment items in the beginning, until I realized that since so many of the ladies who sell here consider this to be their one source of income for themselves.

With that in mind, I decided to start buying them from them at wholesale prices. There are so many primitive stores that you can find online now a days, that finding product wholesale is no longer an issue. And those who have fallen in love with Chocolate Blessings know that they can always find items for their home or as gifts here.

Normally the first few minutes of each Thursday morning is spent pursuing all the new finds within this nook. After that, we gather at the table, get comfy and delve right into each other's lives. For the longest time, my life was the hot topic. Thankfully, no longer! This time it appears to be Tracey's turn. As much as she is one of my closest friends, I take delight in having the focus set on her for a change.

"So Tracey, how are the kids doing? Was Pastor Mike able to take a break from the church office and watch the little ones for you, or did you have to find a sitter?" Judy asked. Tracey was married to Pastor Mike Wells, the youth pastor in our church. They have been with our church for the past four years now, and are loved by many in the church. Tracey has three children. I used to envy her, until I took a few days off and helped around her home after the birth of her youngest. Boy-oh-boy, children are a lot of hard work! Over the past couple months we have been holding Tracey up in prayer. Normally not one to be quiet, lately it seems extra difficult to get her out of the house, to have a smile on her face, or even to join in our study as she used to.

Tracey smiles, "Little Miles is really growing. Hard to believe he's now seven months. He's starting to get the hang of crawling, which means Josiah has to clean up his toys more. Katy is having a bit of a hard time with school. Mike and I have talked about home school; but I honestly don't think it's something I could handle right now," she admits while giving a sheepish grin.

"Home school Tracey! Are you out of your mind? You have little ones at home, is that something you really want to be doing right now?" I exclaim. She seems so worn out lately, this is the last thing she needs to do.

"Well, it's just been a thought Wynne. Mike has talked to a couple families in our church who home school, and they all claim that their children excel more at home. I just don't know," she sighs as she says this.

I feel a kick on my shin and while I'm rubbing it, I see Pastor Joy give me a dirty look. I'm the one who should be handing out the dirty looks; it's my shin that now hurts!

Hmm, perhaps this is her subtle way of telling me to mind my own business. Do you think?! I'm positive that I'm going to have a bruise there in the morning!

"Tracey, would you mind if we brought this to the Lord in prayer? This is obviously something that weighs pretty heavily on your heart, and it's the last thing you need to be worrying about right now," asked Pastor Joy. She's great in hearing what people have to say, and then directing things to God.

As Tracey nods her head in agreement, I notice Joan fiddling in her seat. She keeps twisting the surprise box in her hands and finally blurts out, "Oh come on ladies, lets hurry and open our boxes so we can see what goodies lie inside. I'm sure the good Lord will understand the need to have a bit of heaven in our mouths before we begin!"

"Yes lets! Both Susan and Matt made me promise not to peek inside the boxes, so I can't wait to see what you have!" I explain. One thing I have learnt since opening Chocolate Blessings, I can't taste test all the goodies and not have it affect me! Although I pray on a daily basis the Lord's Prayer, with heavy emphasis on "lead me not into temptation," this is one temptation that I have a hard time resisting. So a few months ago I made a promise to myself to not eat any chocolate (unless sugar free) before noon. It's been a rough go, but I've been able to abstain. Well, ok... I've been able to abstain most of the time.

"Well, we wouldn't want Wynne to break her promise, now would we!" chuckles Judy. So as they all slowly open their surprise boxes, I lean in trying to peek. Inside the boxes, Susan has created a masterpiece! As I hear the "oh's," and "ahh's," I also get to see what is inside. Within each box, Susan has created a basket made out of chocolate. Inside each basket are tiny little chocolate forms. Each appears to be different in design. Judy has a white chocolate basket filled with little chocolate apples. Pastor Joy has a milk chocolate basket filled with little Christmas tree shaped chocolates. Tracey has the same basket but with baby sheep forms, and Joan has a dark

21

chocolate basket filled with chocolate hearts. Susan has truly outdone herself!

As each Latte Lady savors her tiny piece of chocolate heaven, Pastor Joy brings out her Bible and begins to do a little study. We are dealing with how we view ourselves as Daughters of God. It's been an interesting study to say the least. It's one thing to actually say you are a child of God. But it's another thing to believe it. She encourages us and gives us our homework. Yes, homework. The dreadful word that makes all children shudder when they hear it. Yet, as adults, it doesn't bother us as much. We are to spend this next week delving into scripture to find where the Word gives a description of who we are in Jesus. Pastor Joy encouraged us to find a scripture to memorize and to make it personal. My favorite one is in Psalms—"I will not die but live and proclaim what the Lord has done." No matter what happens in my life, I will give God the glory at all times. It was this scripture that helped me to hold my head high after the whole wedding fiasco.

After our prayer at the end where we pray for Tracey, I begin to gather up all the coffee cups and empty chocolate boxes. I hear the jingle of the doorbells ring, and briefly glance to see who has walked in. To my surprise it was Nancy Montgomery. The current bain of my very existence. It is very rare that Nancy comes into Chocolate Blessings.

She blames me for running her son out of town.

I pretend that I didn't see Mrs. Montgomery. Maybe that way she will not notice me and then hopefully leave. Any encounters that I have had with her in the past three years have either almost left me in tears or made me want to scream. I don't know how she does it, but she leaves me quaking in my very shoes.

And to think that she once loved me and was going to be my mother-in-law!

Roses & diamonds
are great gifts indeed...
but to smile each day,
it's chocolate I need.

Chapter 3

"MRS. MONTGOMERY! SO NICE TO SEE YOU! You came at just the right time! We have a new display, called our Sweet Surprise! Don't you think the little boxes with bows are adorable! And just wait till you see what is inside—you won't be able to resist!" chatted Lily. Thank goodness for Lily! As she continues her chatter with Nancy, I try to casually slink away.

Unfortunately, neither slinking nor the chatter worked as a victorious diversion.

"Yes, Lily, I will take one of those boxes, but first I must speak with Wynne. I know she has her little Bible study this morning, so she must be around," answers Nancy as she looks around the store. I know she will spot me any moment, so I stand up straight, grasp Judy's hand for a quick moment of strength, and call out a greeting, which I hope doesn't show my hesitation.

"Good morning Nancy. You'll love what you find in those mystery boxes. Is there anything I can help you with?" I ask as I'm silently congratulating myself for not allowing my voice to quiver.

"Yes, actually there is. Lily, be a dear and ring up a few of those boxes, as well as one of those little gift cards that you have, and have it say Welcome Home. Also, I want that white pitcher in the window display that holds those lovely Gerbera flowers," she requests as she walks towards me.

"Wynne, I have received some news this morning that I wanted to share with you. Jude is coming home today. His father is ill, and he is coming home to help with the business. Please leave him alone. Stay out of his way. My son has finally decided to return home, to where he belongs. You broke his heart once; he doesn't need you to do it again. Stay away from my son," she declares with a cold gleam in her eye.

Ever since that fateful day when I wouldn't walk down the aisle, Nancy Montgomery has blamed me for the fact that her son left town and moved away three years ago. Never mind the fact that it was a mutual agreement not to get married and that it was his decision to move away. She adamantly declares that I broke her son's heart. While I do agree with her, doesn't she see that it hurt me to do it? I understand that she is hurt and feels abandoned by her only child, but why does she continually take it out on me?

Nancy has a habit of giving me the cold shoulder whenever we meet in church. I get the small nod as a greeting. She will go out of her way to avoid me at all costs. Very rarely does she come into my store, yet she always seems to know what is happening in my life. Nancy and I had developed a close relationship once upon a time. Jude was a major part of my life for such a long time that it just became natural to have a relationship with his mother. It was one thing to lose her presence in my life, but it has been quite another thing to be treated as a stranger.

I close my eyes briefly at the news that Jude is coming home. When she first said that he was coming home, I had a brief, very brief, moment of pure joy. Then reality set in. I know the joy of the Lord is to be my strength, but in this instance, I don't feel very strong. For three years I have had to pretend that the break up between Jude and I was mutual, that there were no hard feelings. When he decided to leave town, my heart broke. He is such a great guy, and I broke his heart. Not too many people know what really happened between us. We both agreed it was better that way.

"Nancy, I am sorry to hear that Mr. Montgomery is not well. I will be keeping him in my prayers. It must be a relief to you that Jude is finally coming home," I give her a brief smile. "But Nancy, the only relationship between Jude and I is friendship. I haven't seen him since he left, and although we've remained in touch here and there, I really don't see anything happening between us. We've been over for a long time," I reply. Do I really believe that though? Deep in my heart I know we weren't meant for each other, but I still have feelings for him. Goodness—I almost married the guy, of course I'm still going to have feelings for him

"That is good to hear Wynne. Just make sure you keep it that way," declares Nancy. She begins to move toward the front door. She stops, turns her head and drops her final piece of news. "Jude has moved on with his life. He is even bringing a friend of his home with him for us to meet. He doesn't need you in his life to complicate things," she announces as she walks out the door. The door slams, leaving me with no response.

I feel like I'm about to crumble. Thank goodness I haven't moved away from the tables. I sit down and begin to take some deep breaths. Tracy comes to place her hand on my shoulder. I had completely forgotten that the ladies were still here. Judy takes hold of my hands and gives them a squeeze. Then Joan declares, "I think this is the perfect time for some more chocolate."

Pastor Joy comes over and gives me a brief hug. "I need to leave for the office, but Wynne, please give me a call if you need me! You are a strong woman of God, and you can get through this! I know you," she whispers in my ear, and then she turns to whisper something to Judy before she walks away.

Lily comes over with some chocolate in her hands. I absently take what she offers, only to briefly realize that this is the chocolate that I keep hidden away. This chocolate only comes out in dire need. How does she know about this? I make a mental note to find out later as I savor the sweet decadence melting in my mouth.

With a quick, "Lord, give me strength," prayer being uttered, I stand up and try to act as if nothing was said that should affect me in the way it has. It's a façade, a mask that I try to place on but which never really works with this group of ladies. I give them all a quick smile.

"I'm okay. It has been a long three years. You ladies have helped me to get through this, and I'm okay. I'm glad he's been able to move on with his life. That's the way it should be. And other than seeing him at church," I shrug my shoulders, "I doubt I'll come in much contact with him." Do I really believe what I just said? My favorite saying will come into play right about now.

"After all, with God and chocolate, I can get through anything!"

Each lady gives me a sad little look before they begin to say goodbye and take their leave. I have offers to dinner, coffee and even a chocolate cake, which I accept with gratitude. After all, who can really resist chocolate cake!

I walk back to the counter, absently arranging displays on my way. Lily gives me a look of pity as I walk by her.

"Lily, before we have more customers, can you come to the back and help me bring out some new product that arrived. And don't give me any more of those looks. Jude is a part of my life that is history, and it will stay that way. By the way, how did you know where my secret stash was?" I question as I move into my office. As if I'm going to let this little fact slip by me!

After a busy day consisting of Bible study, mystery boxes, and out of the blue announcements along with the normal hustle and bustle that comes with running a shop, I am wiped out! Since 6 PM when I closed up the store, I have been dreaming of a hot bubble bath. It is now three hours later, and I am just now walking through my front door. That dream will soon become a reality. I have full intentions of ignoring the beeping and flashing light on my answering machine. I am tired, drained and all I want is to soak in hot water, read a good book and go off to bed. Whoever wanted to talk to me could have called the shop if it was important enough. And since it wasn't, it can wait until the morning.

Those were my intentions. The water is running, bubbles have been added and the book has been selected. But of course, I have to check the phone. You just never know who could have called. It's not like I'm expecting anyone from the past to mysteriously drop by, which I'm not, in case you're wondering. I click the button and discover that I could have resisted the machine after all. It was only my mother.

I love my mom, don't get me wrong. But for the past three years she has been 'concerned' that her daughter has chosen the life of single-hood rather than motherhood. Even though I live across town, only a 15-minute drive from where I grew up, my mom has a tendency to crowd me. She doesn't like the fact I live alone. She's proud of me for opening my own store and the fact that it is successful blows both her and dad away. But it's not what she wanted for my life, and so she feels she needs to worry about me. It's not like I plan on staying single for the rest of my life! It's not my chosen way of living let me tell you!

So with a sigh of exasperation, I listen to the message.

"Wynne dear, this is Mom (as if I don't recognize her voice). Listen, I ran into Nancy Montgomery today. She told me the news. Jude is back in town. Isn't that wonderful honey! You just haven't been the same since he left town (no Mom, I've actually learned to be independent), and I know that you both have a lot to catch up on. Listen. I want to invite him over to dinner this week. He was after all part of our family for such a long time. Tell me what night is good for you, and I'll make all the arrangements! Maybe you could even bring over one of those cakes you make to sell in your store? Hmmm? Ok, call me back. Love you." Click.

She has no idea. When it all had happened, I refused to talk about it with her or my father. I asked them to respect my privacy and my decision. And that is how it has been left. But to invite him to dinner? Knowing how emotionally hurt and physically drained I was when he left, she actually wants me to share one of my cakes with him? Nowhere in the Bible does it say I have to share my chocolate cake with my enemies, only that I have to pray for them! I don't share my chocolate with just anybody you know. This is where I draw the line! I shake my head as I head back to my bath. That was definitely a phone call I just didn't need to hear.

To me, having a bath is a luxury that one must never give up. To be able to sink into the hot water and have it completely engulf you is close to heaven! Add scented bubbles, candles all through the room, a cool drink to refresh yourself with and of course a little bit of chocolate to nibble on, and it couldn't get any better! It's the one part of my daily routine that I refuse to give up. Having a hot bath is not only considered a way to pamper yourself, but it also helps you to fall asleep faster. Add a good book, and you're off to far away places, distant lands and pure romance. That is, if your mind behaves itself and goes along with your plans.

Tonight my mind and thoughts decided to rebel. All I could think about was the fact Jude is back in town. I would find myself smiling and giving those little happy sighs when I thought of all the great memories we had. And then all of a sudden I would remember what occurred three years ago, and I would begin to feel anger. Anger that is directed towards God first, and then at myself. This was something I had dealt with; it's not supposed to hurt me anymore. I've laid it at the foot of the cross, and Jesus is supposed to hear all my hearts cries and rescue me. So why isn't that happening? I won't allow myself to dwell on my feelings towards God, after all, who can be mad at God? That's just not allowed. But why now, when I am happy and content with my life, does he have to come back and remind me of my past failures? We were just one of those couples who didn't make it. It happens to a lot of people in relationships. Sometimes you are blessed to have that one deep love, and other times you have to settle for second best. We both decided not to settle. It would have been nice if we could have kept in touch, but I understand that it would have been difficult for him. Plus, from what I understood from Nancy, he has already moved on with his life, and is involved with someone else. That fact alone should make me happy for him. So with that all said, seeing him again shouldn't be too nerve racking. After all, we are all grown adults. Time has gone by, and while feelings might still be there, there's no possibility of them being acted upon.

Basically the enjoyment of my bath ritual was ruined so I went into the kitchen to heat some water for some gourmet hot chocolate. While waiting for the water to boil, I decided to check my email. Perhaps I should unplug the phone just in case Mommy Dearest decided to call back. I definitely am not in the mood for conversation with her tonight.

After my computer loaded up and my email popped up, I made the mistake of clicking into my instant messenger system. Up popped MM2CHOCQUEN (Mom to Chocolate Queen).

> MM2CHOCQUEN: Did you get my message?
> CHOCQUEEN: Yes.
> MM2CHOCQUEN: Why didn't you call back?
> CHOCQUEEN: Was I supposed to?
> MM2CHOCQUEN: What date is good for dinner?
> CHOCQUEEN: I don't want to do dinner, Mom. Sorry.
> MM2COCQUEN: I thought it was a great idea. To get you and Jude together...

CHOCQUEEN: I don't want to get together Mom. Please leave it alone.

MM2COCQUEN: I don't understand you. Why won't you tell me what happened? It's not too late, you know.

CHOCQUEEN: Yes, it is too late. Good night, Mom.

I suppose that if I had explained it all to my parents at the time when he left, this could have been avoided. But knowing my parents, they would have tried to fix the problem. And this was just one problem that could not be fixed.

With a sigh, I shut down my computer, fix my cup of hot chocolate and head to the living room where I plan to shut down my thoughts and relax in front of the television watching either a mindless comedy or a popular drama.

I get all comfy cozy, wrapped in a blanket, fireplace turned on, with my favorite show on and I settle in for a quiet night of relaxation. The doorbell rings. Can I not have a quiet night after having a bit of a stressful day? It had better not be my mother!

I make sure I look in the mirror before I open the door. I am in my pajamas, after all. But I'm decent. That is all that matters. The doorbell rings again. "I'm coming, I'm coming," I call out. I plaster a smile on my face, even though it's the last thing I feel like doing. I open the door. And it is definitely not my mother!

As I glance at my visitor, I blurt out:
"What are you doing here?"

"There's nothing better
than a good friend...
unless it's a good friend
with especially good
chocolate."

~Linda Grayson

Chapter 4

"WHAT DO YOU MEAN, what am I doing here? Is that the way you greet visitors nowadays? What do you think I'm doing here? Our program is on and I brought some munchies. Now get out of the doorway so I can come in before we miss too much!" returned Susan, while shoving me out of the doorway.

"Sorry. I didn't mean to sound rude. I completely forgot that you were coming over tonight," I tried to apologize as I followed behind her to the couch.

"You had better be sorry. I brought your favorites you know. Chewy chocolate chip cookies and ruffled plain chips with dip. But if you keep up with the attitude, I'll just keep the cookies to myself!" replied Susan. She holds the bag of my favorite cookies in front of my nose and teases me mercilessly!

"Oh, you're so tough! Give me those!" I made a grab for the cookies and actually managed to snatch them from her greedy fingers. Imagine the audacity of threatening me with cookies! We each have a good giggle and get comfy with the blankets and goodies.

About half way through the program I decide to broach the subject that I know Susan actually wants to talk about but is being nice enough to wait for me.

"So I guess you heard the news about today?"

"Whew. It's about time you brought it up! I've been impatiently waiting all evening to talk to you about it. How are you doing? Oh, off subject, what did you think of the Sweet Surprise boxes?" Susan asks.

"Hmmm, I loved them! You did an amazing job creating those little chocolate baskets with all the little goodies! Just perfect! I think we should do more of those throughout the year, but I'll order some boxes with windows, so you can see the baskets. You once again outdid yourself! Thank you." I seriously love all her creations. I sincerely believe her gifting is with food. Not one single thing that she makes turns out tasting bad. Me, on the other hand—well, let's just say that I'm not that gifted in the area of cooking. Now baking, that is a different story! Where do you think all the cakes in my store come from?

"Thanks. That's a great idea. I'll have to charge extra next time," Susan says as she gives a little wink.

"Listen, with all that you do, I couldn't even begin to repay you. As Matt says, you're worth your weight in gold!

"But, in all seriousness, I'm ok. Can you imagine Nancy coming up to me like that and telling me to stay away from her son! The claws were visible this time around. She reminded me of a mother bear with her cub. Do I look that dangerous? Seriously, Susan, after everything, does she really think we would be able to pick up right where we left off? I don't think so! Besides, from what I understood, he's already involved, and more than likely hasn't given me one moment of his thoughts. But why should he? He's the one who ran away rather than face the music and try to work things out." I'm babbling. I almost sound like it matters to me, after all this time.

"Methinks the lady doth protest too much!" says Susan.

"Hmm, it sounds that way doesn't it? But it doesn't matter though, does it?" I said, with a hint of sadness starting to settle in. Do I allow my heart's hurts to surface, or should I just shrug them off again and pretend it doesn't bother me? With Susan, I don't have to worry about hiding things. And even if I did, she knows me too well. She knows the whole story after all.

"Wynne, I really think it would be helpful if you could talk to Jude about it all. Bring it out in the open and face the issues. It doesn't matter if it's in the past. It's a part of who you are. You need closure. Then you can finally feel free to move on with your life. You guys made the right decision, so stop beating yourself up about it. It's time you invested some time into a man, into your future, something other than Chocolate Blessings," encouraged Susan.

"Hmmm, we'll have to see. Right now, I don't think it would make much difference. We have become one of those casual acquaintances that have a bit of a history. We'll be the type of people who are able to say hi without too much awkwardness," I replied, without too much conviction, if I'm going to be honest.

"Well, I'm sure it will all work out. You might even be a bit surprised at the outcome. I'm here for you nonetheless. Anyways, I've been thinking. We need to plan a girls' night out! I think Tracey could really use it, and it's been awhile since we've actually done anything fun," Susan expressed while grabbing another cookie.

"Oh, that will be fun! Where should we go? How about Mama Rose's? Or grab a chick flick at the theatre? Do you think we can convince Tracey to actually join us? Last time we tried to plan a girls' night, she cancelled on us last minute, remember?" I mentioned to her.

After Tracey's last baby, it seems like she's had a hard time finding enjoyment in life. Having three children has to be tiring, but it seems to be more than that. A couple months ago Susan and I had the brilliant idea that Tracey needed to have a night with no kids. We planned a dinner and shopping spree. Yet, at last minute, Tracey cancelled, using the excuse that the baby was being fussy and she didn't feel right leaving him with Mike.

"Matt has already spoken with Mike, and he's working on clearing a night from his calendar so that he can be home with the kids. As soon as he lets us know, we'll go and literally kidnap Tracey so that she doesn't have time to think of an excuse," Susan plotted.

I began to giggle. "Ohhh, you sound so sinister!" I laughed at her. Out of all my friends, Susan has the wildest imagination around!

Susan just laughed with me before she began to gather her things together.

"Now, it's time to go home. I'll let you keep the few cookies that are left. Don't think about Jude too much tonight, ok Wynne? No sense worrying about something you can't handle until it's actually hitting you in the face. I'll be in the store tomorrow, so I'll see you then," says Susan.

As I walk Susan to the door, I realize that this is going to be one long night for me. Do I seriously think that I will be able to just ignore the fact that the one guy that I did the unspeakable to has now returned? I once swore that I would never hurt someone in that way. I know how heart breaking, soul tossing that is. Can I ignore the fact that this is one issue

I've never really dealt with, only because it would mean I would have to face the real issues that I have with God?

I think I need to grab those cookies and any other chocolate that I can find in my house and indulge. All I can say is that these cookies had better be fat free! There's no way I'm gaining any weight over my feelings for a man! Dear Diary, here I come.

I looked out the window to see the sun shining, snow glistening like sparkling diamonds, children laughing as they build snowmen, and see the thermometer outside my window reading a balmy −18. Brrrrrrr. Why is it that children never seem to mind the cold while adults always dread it? I bundle up nice and warm with a thick sweater, my parka, wooly mitts, scarf and hat, grab the chocolate cake that I finished making early this morning and head out to my car.

The whole way down the stairs and across the walkway I find myself saying a double prayer. "Lord please let my car start this morning, and please let me make it to my car without falling!" I should be wearing my ice skates, either that or ski down the path to my car. If I can make it in one piece this morning without the cake becoming an upside down creation, I will be happy. "I promise to smile to all those I meet (even though my lips might crack due to the cold), I will play Christmas music all day, and I'll even make chocolate chip cookies for my next door neighbor who gives me all those mean looks when I come home late in the evening and put on my favorite worship CD nice and loud. If only I make it in one piece!"

Do you think making those types of deals with God really works? Should I include the fact that I'll even try to not eat chocolate today if I make it in one piece? Do you think He will hear me and answer my prayer?

Wait a minute; did I really almost say that I'd not eat chocolate today? That's barely possible, not a concept that my brain can even begin to comprehend, let alone dwell on! I think I need more coffee. No, let me rephrase that. I definitely need more coffee!

I love the routine of opening up the store. I get to see the store in its glory, quiet, clean and well stocked, just waiting for customers to come in and fall in love with all the delicious treats. When the first aroma of coffee begins to drift through the store, then I know it's time to open. I decided long ago that it is against my policy to have a customer walk into our store and not be greeted by the fresh aroma of brewed coffee and chocolate. I mean, who in their right minds could start their day without those essentials?

I like to have a Flavor of the Week, something that is a new creation for me. I sell this as a product and as a ready-made beverage. This week I decided to make Dreamy Swiss Mocha Coffee Mix. I hit the jackpot this summer when I discovered boxes of decorative tins at a flea market in a nearby town. I have been using these tins for an assortment of gift ideas. This week it has been to hold the dry mix of Dreamy Swiss Mocha Coffee. Add some ribbon, a little card detailing instructions on how to make the coffee, and it becomes a perfect gift idea. The recipe for this mix is really simple. All you need is:

2 c. coffee-mate	2 c. unsweetened cocoa
1 c. instant coffee crystals	2 c. sugar
1 tsp. nutmeg	1 tsp. cinnamon

Mix all ingredients together. For an individual cup, add 2-¾ tsp. hot water. Top with whipped cream and sprinkle with nutmeg. Voila—the perfect way to begin each day. All that you need to add is your favorite muffin, and you are set!

For the store, I like to prepare this in a large slow cooker, and have it simmering all day. I offer this free, as a taste test to indulge the senses. Very rarely can a customer not buy the tin as a gift, whether for his or her own personal use or for someone they love.

As I am getting the cake I made last night ready for display, my first customer walks through the door. I like to make the first customer of the day feel extra special, so I always have a piece of chocolate ready for them to take home along with a rose. This policy has gotten around a bit, and there will be times when it's a race to the counter in the mornings if a group of ladies walk in.

"Good morning! Thank you for coming in this morning! I have a fresh pot of Swiss Mocha on this morning, please help yourself. My name is Wynne, and if there is anything I can do to help you, please don't hesitate to let me know!" I called out as a greeting. I don't recognize the woman who walked in, so I know she's not a regular. It's quite early this morning for a non-regular to grace Chocolate Blessings.

She gives me a bit of a funny look, but replies nonetheless.

"Thank you. Something definitely smells wonderful! I saw this store last night as we drove into town. I love gourmet coffee, and when I saw your sign, I knew this would be the perfect place to come for my coffee," my guest replied as she began to walk through the store and examine all the displays and hangings on the walls.

"There is a little corner where the coffee is, so feel free to sit, relax and enjoy your morning treat," I explained as I continued to set up the cake. I take a few peeks at my guest. She is tall, blond and really quite beautiful. I never would have guessed that she liked chocolate. But then, what woman could honestly resist chocolate!

As my guest walks through the store, in walks Tracey, sans her children. You could tell she was in 'get me away' mode, for as soon as she walked into the store she took a deep breath, and a sigh of relief escaped her mouth at the same time. I've often seen this happen to mothers of young children. They put all their effort into just trying to get away for a little while, that once they actually are able to make their great escape, it almost seems unreal to them. I love to watch it. There are days when I desperately cry out for a child of my own, and then there are days when I watch some mothers that I decide it would be better to just be happy and satisfied with my lot in life.

"Good morning Tracey! You look like you need a strong cup of coffee and a special treat to go with it! How about a lemon poppy seed muffin? I stopped at the bakery this morning, and Diane was just pulling these out of the oven, so you know that they will be still warm," I suggest with a smile on my face. She really does look like she needs to get away for a while.

"Wynne. My angel in disguise! Would you mind if I took my muffin, coffee and book and curled myself up in one of your comfy chairs for, oh I don't know, a few years? Perhaps even decades?" Tracey declares as she pours her coffee.

"Um, no, but I might need to start charging you a sitting fee! Go on over, curl up and enjoy some quiet. I'll come over in a bit and join you for coffee."

"Thanks so much. You're a sweetie. But just to warn you... give me a good half hour or more before you come over! I need that much time just to cool down!" she warned as she headed over to the comfy section of the café.

I chuckle as I watch her head away from me. Tracey and I have been friends forever it seems. I was there when she first met Mike, her husband. At the time she was adamant about never marrying a pastor. I think we were both of the same mind. I mean, who would actually want to be married to a man who has to spend more time at the church than at his own home, or else the "sheep" begin to complain. A man who not only has to preach a sermon at least three times a week, but do counseling, plus hospital visits, plus home visits, not to mention the countless hours driving to those visits. I remember watching our senior pastor's wife while I was growing up. I always thought that not only did she marry the pastor, but she also married the ministry, and all the headaches associated with it. It would take a special kind of person to do that, and neither Tracey nor myself figured we could do it.

Growing up, Tracey was the type of girl you always looked up to. She was smart, challenging, fun, strong, and always had a goal set out before her. Our joined image in what a pastor's wife should look like definitely was not Tracey. We had both made a pact that we would be women who changed the world, not have the world change them. We were going to conquer all that came our way. Someone had once suggested that we both go to Bible College, to get some good training on how to be a perfect wife. Can you imagine the audacity! Instead, I went to college and took English literature. I eventually dropped out when I realized that English literature was not my heart's passion. Tracey went on to become an accountant. Blah and boring you might think, but she is a whiz when it comes to numbers! In her second-last year she met Mike at a church service. Long story short, they fell in love, she left me to marry him, never finished her degree and instead began to have babies. When she met Mike, he was finishing his degree at Bible College and had high aspirations of changing today's youth. Despite all our vows and promises, Tracey became that dreaded pastor's wife. She was happy though. Surprisingly, motherhood fulfilled a dream within her heart that neither one of us knew she had.

Throughout the past few years she has had more babies, three in total, and I have watched her slowly fall into a depression. She thinks I actually believe her when she tells me it's the Baby Blues she is experiencing. Normally, I would tend to agree, but this has been going on for a long time. I pray for her, and hope that one day she will open up enough to share what is really going on. Until then, I will be the best friend that I can be by offering her what I know she wants—unlimited chocolates!

While I'm dwelling on my good friend, my unknown customer walks up to the counter. She beams me a smile that I just can't help but return.

"Wynne, is it?" she asked hesitantly. After I nodded she continued.

"I love your store! So many treats to choose from. And all the talent that you portray here! You offer a variety from the primitive style to the shabby chic look. Perhaps you can help me a little?" she asks while she turns her gaze to the floor and begins to fidget a little bit with her hands.

"I am a guest in someone's home and I would like to buy her a gift. I'm having a hard time choosing, and was hoping that you might be familiar with her," she continued.

"Not a problem! Perhaps if you tell me her name, we can figure out something for her together," I suggested while she gave me a sheepish look.

"Oh sure, I um, thought you would have known. Sorry. It's Mrs. Montgomery. Jude's mother," she told me with an apologetic tone in her voice.

All of a sudden you could feel the awkward air surround us. So this must be Jude's new friend. Well, he definitely has moved on with his life! Now how do I respond to this? I think it's safe to assume that things must be pretty serious between them for him to bring her home, so any thoughts of resurrecting our past (if I had any to begin with) have now gone down the drain. Do I suck it up and act like a mature adult, or could I be just a bit vindictive and play with her a little bit? Of course I'll do the Christian thing and be the nice lady who doesn't hold any grudges, especially against someone who can't help what has happened.

"Of course I know Nancy. She was just in here yesterday to tell me that Jude was coming home and that a friend was joining him. I'm assuming you're that friend? I'm sorry, I didn't catch your name though." Did that come out too harsh? Too abrupt?

"I'm Stacey. Stacey Lawd. Jude mentioned that you owned a store, but I didn't realize it was this one," she said a bit apologetically. Hmmm, so she wouldn't have come in if she actually knew that this was my store. Interesting!

"I passed by on my walk this morning and just had to stop in. I really like your store. You look like you've done really well, despite this being a small town. So, do you think you can help me find a gift? I think it's safe to assume that you know Nancy a bit better than I do." She suddenly turned a nice shade of pink. So she finds this awkward as well. Hmmm. Very intriguing! While Stacey was mentioning her quest for that perfect gift for Nancy, I couldn't help but notice the absence of a ring on her finger. Ah, the awkwardness of getting to know the parents! She must still be in the stages of getting Nancy to like her. I do feel for her. It can be quite the daunting task! I was once in her shoes, so I should know.

"Well of course I can help you. I was once in your shoes, as I'm sure you've heard. Nancy isn't the easiest of women to please, but she does seem to love this store," I admit to her.

"Tell you what," I continued, "let's just get all the awkwardness out of the way, shall we? I was once engaged to Jude, broke his heart, he left town and we have kept in touch here and there. I'm his past, he's my past, and it will stay that way. I'm assuming you are his girlfriend, and it must be pretty serious if he brought you home. So, since we have so much in common, we'll use that as our common purpose and not let all the other garbage get in the way!" That was quite bold and daring for me. But one thing I have learned over the years is that if you use honesty to your advantage, you can never go wrong. In this case I figure that if I've never met a chocolate I didn't like, that has to be true for friends as well. Besides, if I just assume everyone I meet will become a good friend, then how can I go wrong?

"Phew! That's a relief! I was a bit nervous, if you couldn't tell, about meeting you. I told Jude this morning that it doesn't matter what happened between the two of you. It hasn't affected me in any way, nor am I going to let it affect me. I'm so glad that I ran into you this morning! Now, give me some ideas for his mom," Stacey replied.

Instead of the awkwardness that surrounded us earlier, it now feels the opposite. She seems like she is a breath of fresh air. I'm already beginning to like her. And the fact that she finds Nancy a challenge, without coming right out and saying it, that says something to me. She's a smart cookie.

"Well, why don't I give you several ideas, and then let you make the decision. I've noticed that she is beginning to collect things that are white. Especially accessories. Yesterday she was in and bought a white pitcher with some Gerbera flowers in it. She loves chocolate, stationary and candles." I list off a few suggestions to her, hoping that she will have already noticed a few items that caught her eye.

"I'm pretty sure that white pitcher with the flowers is now in my room. It's gorgeous! And I love the flowers! So cheery and bright. What about some of those wall wreaths? Or do you think that might be too inappropriate for right now?" Stacey asked in a questioning statement.

"Hmm, I have noticed her admiring them before, but—and this is just my personal suggestion—how about doing up a little basket with a few things in it. That way it's not too overpowering, and you know she will fawn over it all. We have some vintage milk candlesticks or vases, a few votives, a pad of stationary, perhaps a doily or tea towel for the kitchen. Or it could be a themed basket? Take a look around and let me know if you need any more help," I suggested. I had a few more customers walk into the store and I needed to focus some attention on them.

"I love the idea of a themed basket. Thanks! I'll just take a look around, and let you get back to work, thanks Wynne," was

Stacey's comment as she began to wander throughout the store again.

I have to admit that Stacey doesn't seem too bad. I don't know what I was expecting. In my head I had visions of the 'unknown' lady friend coming up to me and giving me a good ole' chick slap, right across my face, in revenge for hurting her dearly beloved. She would walk away with refined dignity, and I would be left standing there, with a red cheek, feeling utter amazement and embarrassment. Not a pretty sight, and definitely not the type of daydream that I like to have! It is nice though to know that I'm not the only one in this lifetime who is a bit nervous when it comes to Nancy. I shake my head. I am definitely glad I'm not in those shoes anymore. So glad, in fact, that I think I could celebrate with a little piece of a chocolate slowpoke right about now.

It would be nice to be left in la-la land for a little while, just me and my own thoughts and weird daydreams, but I was rudely brought out of my reverie by an insistent voice that was mentioning my chocolate cake.

"Wynne, the perfect sight for the perfect morning! Look at that cake you made! It looks absolutely delicious! Do you think it's too early to have a slice now? Oh and look at the pretty little pink rosebuds. I would have to say that the cake-decorating course you took last year has definitely paid off. A beautiful showcase! Well, since it's too early to have some cake—and what a shame that is—I'll just have to enjoy your Dreamy Swiss Mocha. And of course I will take a tin of it! Wherever did you find those tins? I love them! I think you should create a display of them and sell them. They would definitely be a hot item around here. You just know how much everyone loves these cute tins. Antique aren't they? I think my mother used to have a bunch of these when I was just a wee little lass. Now those were the days! No frills, just plain honest hard work and simplicity. That's what got us through the day. But then, I wasn't allowed to have chocolate for breakfast either... so on that note, I think I will have a slice of your cake!" ended Joan with a note of triumph to her voice. And I agree with her. Having chocolate cake for breakfast is quite the accomplishment!

"Joan, did you even take a breathe during that whole speech? You bring a smile to my face!" which is true, since the moment she began I couldn't stop smiling. "To answer your question, I found those tins at a garage sale last year. I might be able to part with a few of them, but I really like the idea of using them for my Flavored Coffees. And just because you are my favorite customer, how about an extra big slice of cake! You'll need it to get through the day, and you know that I pray all the calories out of these cakes while I'm making them!" I like to spoil Joan. She is one of my favorite Latte Ladies. Sometimes it doesn't always hurt to treat someone as if they were just a little extra special, especially when it happens to be true.

"Well thank you, my dear girl! You certainly know how to make one's day! Now, I do believe that is Tracey I see over there sitting by herself this morning. I think she needs a good ole mama hug! Now don't you be shaking your head at me. No, no, don't tell me to leave her alone. You can see that she is one hurting girl, and when the Lord told me to come over here this morning, I knew it was for a reason. That girl over there just needs to be reminded that she is loved!" and with that, Joan took off over to Tracey.

Joan is one of those sweet women who go about each day fully trusting in God to lead her. She believes that God orders the steps of a righteous man, or woman in her case, and she is determined to walk each step the way God would have her. That being said, she is very sensitive, in all her quirkiness, to when people just need a bit of encouragement. Where I tend to just stand back and give them space when they have asked for it, Joan will just walk right into that space that they hold on to so dearly and give them a hug.

As I watch Joan give Tracey a hug without spilling her goodies, I say a quick prayer for them both. This is just one more reason why I love my Latte Ladies group so much.

From the corner of my eye I notice Stacey coming back towards me with her arms full of items for her basket. I casually go through what she has picked and I have to admit, she has excellent taste. She went with a kitchen theme. With that in mind, she had compiled hand soap, tarts and a tart burner, kitchen scented candles, homespun tea towels, a little plaque that has embroidered "Give us this day our daily bread" within it, a coffee mug, white water pitcher and a box of chocolates.

"I like your selections Stacey. I think she will definitely like what you picked out. Not too overbearing, with some personal touches in there. I like it. Would you like me to arrange it and wrap it up?" I asked as I rang up her order.

"Hmm, you think it's ok? I just tried to think of things my mom might like. I don't want it to look like I'm trying too hard. And I love your coffee! Do you have any of the mix already made up? Oh, right in front of my eyes! Oops. Can you add one of these? It tastes so good!" she added while I began to wrap it all together.

After a bit of casual chitchat concerning the store, our love for chocolate, etc., just as Stacey was ready to leave, the bell above my door began to jingle. I had just bent down behind my shelf to retrieve a bag for the basket when I heard his voice.

"There you are! I thought maybe you had gotten lost on your walk and came to find you. I almost didn't notice you from the window. Are you ready to go?" the voice belonged to, yep, you guessed it. Jude.

I take a deep breath. If I hid down here long enough, do you think they would just leave? Do I really have to stand up? Do you know how silly I must look? I lift up my head, and all I see are four sets of eyes staring down on me. Great. Just great.

"Here it is. I knew I had a bag down there large enough for your basket," I nervously chattered away while trying to hide my embarrassment. This was definitely not how I wanted to see Jude for the first time in over three years. Sure we've talked here and there, but I haven't actually seen him since that morning of our wedding.

In my mind I had it played out that I might see him from a distance at church, or maybe walking down the street. We would casually say hi, how are you, nice to see you again, and continue on our way. I, of course would look great, with my hair all done up nice, fresh lipstick on, and clothes to show that I have lost weight since he was last here. But nope. Why can't life actually be like my dreams?

"Jude, well stranger, nice to see you again," oh why couldn't I just have said hi.

"Hey Wynne. So this is your store? Mom mentioned you opened up one, but she made it sound like a hobby store. This looks great," replied Jude. Should I be surprised that Nancy would belittle my passion? No, I'll just let that pass by.

I take a good look at him. He looks great. Tall, still has a small frame, but he looks like he's been working out, so he's a bit more muscular. He still has those soft blue eyes that just make a girl want to daydream. He looks great in his tan sweater with dark blue jeans. He's obviously still impartial to the cold weather since he has his coat slung over his arm. Where most people would be bundled up since it is winter, Jude used to just walk around in a thick sweater with a scarf wrapped around him. His arm is across Stacey shoulder, as if he's trying to show that he's taken, like that would really matter to me. They look great together, though. I give a wistful sigh, and realize with a jolt that he is still talking to me while I'm daydreaming. Again.

"Welcome to Chocolate Blessings," I interrupted. To make it look like I did actually hear him, I threw out my arms in a wide arch, as a way to introduce my store to him. In the process of doing this, I remembered that I had just finished arranging a display of tins with the Swiss Mocha right beside me on the top of the display counter. Before I could even begin to stop myself, my one arm swept across the display case, catching the tins in the process. While I'm slowly moaning "oh no," I watch the tins, as if in slow motion, topple from the counter onto the floor. One decides to become aerobic and bounces from the top of the pile, onto the counter, and then onto me. The bounce from the counter caused the lid to come off, allowing the mocha mix to escape the tin and converge onto my new black sweater. Great, just great! I heave a big sigh, while trying to smile and not look embarrassed at the same time. I decide to take the graceful way out, and hand Stacey her bag, praying fervently under my breath that they will leave. Soon. Like, as in now.

Jude starts to laugh. Stacey begins to giggle. I just stand there, slightly dazed, when the humor of this situation hits me. I join in on the laughing. From the corner I hear Joan yelling "She's at it again," and from that moment on I'm lost. I have to grab the edge of the counter, I'm laughing so hard. An awkward situation becomes humorous. It's all at my expense, but then, what else is new?

"It's nice to know not all things have changed, Wynne," Jude manages to utter in between his laughs. He takes Stacey's bag and leads her to the front door. As they are walking, Stacey calls out from over her shoulder.

"Wynne, it was certainly nice meeting you! A bit interesting maybe, but it was nice. Thanks so much," she said as she waved her purse in the air. And with that they left me standing there not believing what had just occurred.

"Life is like a box of
chocolates—you never know
what you're going to get."

~Forest Gump

Chapter 5

"WYNNE. HI, IT'S ME, TRACEY. It's Friday night, kids are in bed, Mike is working on a sermon, and I'm in the mood for a chick flick. If I bring the movie and popcorn, will you supply the coffee, chocolate and blankets? Give me a call when you get in!" Beep. The only message on my machine! Whew. I'm not usually hesitant to listen to my messages, but with the way the past few days have been going, I have no idea who could be calling.

I think watching a chick flick with a girlfriend is an excellent way to end a horrible day like the one I had today. After Jude and Stacey left the store, I had to endure teasing from Tracey and Judy. It's bad enough that I felt utterly embarrassed, but to listen to others enjoying my humiliation was more than I could handle! After about ten minutes of their teasing and repeating the story to new customers as they walked in, I ordered those two wisecrackers out of my store. I threatened to banish them if they repeated the story of my humiliation to one more person. I'm not sure if it worked or not, since they ended up leaving the store with tears of laughter rolling down their faces, but at least I felt better.

All day I had people who I thought were my friends coming into the store—not to offer me sympathy, but rather, wanting more details. Can you imagine! I don't understand these people. The man I nearly married, but instead ended up breaking his heart, finally comes back into town after three years. My first time seeing him includes having to meet his new girlfriend and making a complete fool of myself. That being said, I did end up selling a lot of product though, since I made everyone who needled me for details buy something from the store, whether it be chocolate, candles, or coffee. No one seemed to mind, which was good. After a long and tiring day, I just wanted to go home and relax. I dreaded the thought of having a full answering machine, thinking that those who didn't come into the store would call wanting details, but thankfully, the only message was Tracey's. But then, that's small town life for you. No one is a stranger, and you always know when someone sneezes.

After I called Tracey back to let her know I was game for our chick night, I decided to indulge and make a pan of hot fudge brownies. These have become my absolute favorite, and something that I don't make for the store. I had come to realize about a year ago that I needed to keep some things sacred to only me. So smoothies, Pina Colada's (made from home with no alcohol) and hot fudge brownies are now my prized possessions. I only share them with a few sacred friends. It's been a while since Tracey and I have had one of those good ole chick nights, so I figure this is a special enough occasion to indulge ourselves.

With the Pina Colada mix ready and the beeper on my oven about to go off, the doorbell rings.

"Come on in," I yell. "I'm in the kitchen." I assume it is Tracey. The beeper on the oven goes off, so I hear a voice calling to me, but can't quite understand the words.

"You're just in time! Our drink is ready, and the brownies are fresh out of the oven warm! Now all we need is the popcorn, and our chick night can begin! What movie did you bring?" I began my monologue with my back turned to the doorway. At the moment I am wearing my flannel pajamas with my "I'm so sexy" apron and my big fuzzy pink princess slippers. With it being girls' night, flannel and fuzzy slippers only seemed appropriate!

"Hmm, I don't think a chick night is exactly my thing, but thanks anyways," was the answer that I received. I froze. That voice did not belong to sweet, feminine Tracey. Rather, it was a deep, and definitely masculine, Jude. Once again, this is not the way that I wanted to see him. Not in flannels, apron and slippers. Not with me bending over my stove door, face flushed. I straightened up slowly, carefully placed the brownies onto my counter and tried to halfway compose myself.

"Um, no. Chick night definitely would not suit you. Sorry, I um, thought you were Tracey," I replied rather apologetically. I was embarrassed. And a little bit unnerved. I didn't quite expect to have Jude walk into my home.

"This is a nice place you have Wynne. It feels homey, and, well, you. It looks like you created what you always desired—a home," commented Jude while he looked around my kitchen/dining area.

"Yes, I have done that. It's not complete yet, but one day," I answered as I reaffirmed my dream to him. To make my home complete, I desire to have a husband and lots of children fill it. I don't know how that will come about, but it will. Of this I am sure.

I was able to buy my dream home a few years ago. It is an older style home, complete with hard wood floors, old wood details around the door frames and windows, old furnace heaters in every room and wood sliding doors between my living room and dining area. It was a bit run down when I bought it, thus enabling me to get a good deal, but with a lot of work it looks amazing! I've decorated it with the sparse look. A little bit of shabby chic meets the primitive look. It doesn't suit everyone's taste, but I love it. And it doesn't hurt that a lot of my accessories come from my store, either!

"So, Jude, what brings you by? I know I've always told you that you're more than welcome to come for a visit, but I never thought you would take me up on it. And where is Stacey? Does she trust you alone with me?" Ok, ok, I admit there was a bit of sarcasm in that last comment. I should apologize, but I won't.

"Be nice Wynne. I didn't think you would mind me dropping by, and I thought we should talk. As for Stacey, she knows where I am and why. I left her with my mom going through those dreaded photo albums that all mothers seem to bring out at the wrong times. I needed to get out and thought to come over here. I hope you don't mind me not calling first. Although," and he is looking me up and down when he says this, "maybe I should have called first."

"Hey—it's not my fault you caught me like this, and there's nothing wrong with how I'm dressed! Tracey is due to come by soon, and we're having a girls' night. Sorry, but no boys allowed," I answered back.

"Alright, I won't stay, but can you spare a few moments to talk? There's something I want to tell you, and I thought you should hear it from me first." Oh no. Those dreaded words. Don't they just send a shiver down your back when you hear them? He's going to tell me he's engaged. I just know it. And why it bothers me, I'm not sure, but it does. It does a lot.

"I plan on asking Stacey to marry me tonight. I thought that with all that we have been through, that you deserved to hear it from me first," was the answer I received.

It hurts. I mask my face so that it doesn't show. I take a deep breath, and plaster the largest smile I've ever had to fake onto my face!

"Congratulations! Wow. I'm... happy for you Jude. That is great. Stacey seems like a great person, and, well, I'm happy for you." Did that sound fake, I wondered, even while I said it?

"Are you really Wynne? I know it shouldn't matter, but it does. Part of me feels bad for finally having found someone I love with all my heart, while you are still, well, you're still here. Waiting. I just wanted, no I needed, well; I'm not sure why I wanted you to know first. I know we once had something special, but I couldn't stand knowing that I would always take second place in your heart, Wynne. I finally realized what you meant by not taking second best. We would have been good for each other, but you're right. We would have been settling. I don't feel I'm settling with Stacey. She's the absolute best. I love her. I hope you can be happy for me?" asked Jude as he looked at me with those big puppy dog eyes. I never could refuse him anything when he looked at me that way, and I told him so now.

"Oh, stop looking at me like that! Of course I'm happy for you! I'm glad that you found someone that you don't feel you're settling with. She must be very special to have claimed your heart, Jude. I'm happy for you! I'll admit it's a hard pill to swallow. You are going to have what I always dreamed of having. And you're not going to have it with me. I think I always thought that once I could let go of the past, that once I gave up that dream I have, you would be the one to have me with open arms. I am happy for you. You're moving on with your life while I'm stuck living in the past," I replied in honesty as I turned away from him to hide my tears. I might be honest to a fault, but I don't need to share my one weakness with everyone.

I could feel Jude come closer to me and hesitantly place his arms around me, giving me a hug. I stiffen up immediately; after all, it's been three years since I was last in this position. But I gradually begin to feel safe and let myself relax a bit as tears continue to run down my face. It feels nice to be in a man's arms again, even if he isn't my man.

I take a big breath and gently step away from the embrace. It's a good thing I did, for at the same time I hear my front door open and close, with Tracey calling out a greeting as she comes through the door.

Jude steps away slowly until he's back leaning against the kitchen counter. I quickly wipe away my tears and try to appear busy while I compose myself. With a quick look to Jude, I call out to Tracey.

"In here, Tracey. In the kitchen." Before I can begin to warn her that Jude is here, Tracey calls out while she's walking.

"Hmmm, something smells good! Please tell me you made the..." She falters as she enters the kitchen. She looks from me to Jude and back again. "...brownies," she finishes a bit lamely.

"Hey, Tracey. Nice to see you again. I just came by to talk with Wynne. But I'll scoot now since I know you guys have other plans that don't include men," greets Jude as he offers a bit of a goofy smile.

"Jude. Hi. You're definitely the last person I expected to see today. But hey, you're looking good! So... before you skiddaddle, what did you have to talk to Wynne about that couldn't wait until your girlfriend was around?" Tracey said in her rather abrupt tone. Tracey is a bit of a mother hen. She likes to protect those she loves. I know she can tell I've been crying, so her feathers are now all in a ruffle.

"I ah, er, well, um, I had some news to share with her," Jude managed to stammer out. I think Tracey caught him a bit off guard with her abruptness.

"And what type of news would that be? Does it affect her at all? And what type of news would you have to share that Stacey couldn't be here..." Tracey slowly stopped, cluing into what that news could be.

"Yep, you guessed it, Tracey" I began. I decided to try and rescue the situation a bit here.

"Jude is..."

"I am..."

We both began at the same time, and stopped at the same time.

"It's your news Jude, you share it," I offered.

57

"I am going to ask Stacey to marry me, and I wanted to tell Wynne before she heard it from someone else," Jude explained to Tracey.

"And I'm so thrilled," I interjected, "that I'm going to throw them an engagement party!" Now where in the world did that come from? Me and my big mouth!

"You are?" both Jude and Tracey said together. And both sounded a little bit shocked.

"I am," I answered with a ring of finality to it. After all, it might be a good decision in the long run. This way none of the busybodies of our town will talk about poor Wynne, the jilted (in their eyes) bride.

"I am. Doesn't that sound like a splendid idea? After all, I love parties, and I love to throw them! Why shouldn't I do this? I want to, plus it will stop all the gossip about my supposedly broken heart if I do this!" I explain. Ok, so maybe I am beginning to sound a bit desperate with my explanation, but there's no way I'm going to be talked out of this now.

"Ok," begins Tracey with a bit of hesitancy in her voice. "Ok, so you, Jude, are getting married, and you, Wynne, are throwing an engagement party. All right. It sounds a bit... hmm, weird, but then you both were always a bit weird together, so who am I to argue? Congratulations, by the way, Jude. I'm assuming your soon to be fiancé was the gal you found in Wynne's store this morning. Stacey, right? Good for you." Tracey stops as she begins to walk toward Jude in the kitchen.

"Now, it is girls' night, and Wynne's famous brownies are done, and the smell is calling to me. I think it's time you left, and we'll all deal with," and she waves her hands around, "whatever just happened here, in the morning," Tracey finished as she begins to scoot Jude out of my kitchen.

While Tracey is gently prodding Jude out of my house, I find myself rooted to the spot on my floor. I can't move. I think I'm in a bit of shock. Did he really just tell me that he's getting engaged? Did I really just say that I would throw him an engagement party? Did I really just share my heart with him concerning my feelings? Is there any possibility that I could be dreaming right now?

I'm still standing in the same spot when Tracey comes back into the kitchen. I lift my head to look her in the eyes. I find myself begin to tear up again, and as she gently enfolds me in her arms, I begin to bawl like a little blubbering baby.

After a few minutes, I am able to compose myself and lift my head. With a smile on my face, I offer the following suggestion.

"Lets eat the brownies, have our drink and enjoy our chick night shall we?"

We made a pact with one another. We would enjoy our movie and snacks before we got into any of the heavy conversations that we both knew would follow. *As if* we could just not talk about what happened, or the reason why she was not only in the store this morning for a time out, but also here at my house tonight for the same reason.

After refills of our special Pina Colada drink, another plate of brownies and our sanity being satisfied with our chick flick, we both took up opposite sides of the couch and settled in for some interesting girly talk. Up for discussion at this moment was the scene earlier in my kitchen.

"I still say we should have a coin toss for who goes first," I began. I'm not sure I really want to delve into the why's of my reactions just yet. I'd rather sink my teeth into what is going on inside Tracey at the moment.

"Don't think I'm going to let you get away with not talking about Jude! Wynne Taylor, I think what happened tonight is a bit more important than the problems I'm having in my marriage. Those will always be there, so it's not all that important," Tracey began to admonish me. I knew deep down that she needed to talk, but maybe she wasn't ready yet.

"Alright, alright. I'll be the self-sacrificing friend, and allow you to dissect me and my reactions. Only for now, though! Don't think you're getting out of this any time soon missy!" I replied, wiggling my finger in front of her face.

"Should I lay down here while you analyze me?" I ask while I proceed to stick my tongue out at her.

"Don't be saucy, or I might just eat up the rest of the brownies! Now, what in all of God's green earth possessed you to agree to hold his engagement party? Why would you do that?" she asked with a tone of incredibility to her questions.

"Well, if you remember correctly, he didn't ask me. I volunteered. And as to why... I'm not sure exactly, but the more I think about the idea, the more I like it! Come on... think about it, Tracey. If I do this for them, then no one will be able to look at me with pity in their eyes, or think that I'm just trying to put on a good face rather than show everyone how broken they think my heart truly is. Isn't that perfect or what?" I explained to her.

"Or what! Seriously Wynne. Think about this! You were once going to marry that man! I was there, I saw it all. You were wearing your wedding dress, the music was playing and you were ready to walk down that aisle and become Mrs. Jude Montgomery. Then all of a sudden, poof, there is Jude at the door demanding to speak with you, and he orders all of your good friends, including your bewildered parents, out of the room so the two of you can talk. Next thing we know, we're being told the wedding is off, Jude has split for who knows where and you are left sitting on the floor in a puddle of tears! No one can forget that day Wynne—least of all you. And now you expect everyone to be happy and to accept that you are throwing him an engagement party! That is not going to fly! Everyone is going to think you're just being the good old Christian martyr that you are, and while you have a good face on, you're crying inside. Come on, now, girl!" explained Tracey while I tried to look anywhere but her. Ok, ok, so what she had to say did make some sense.

"Oh, all right," I sighed, "but you are one of the few people who actually knows what transpired that day. So you should know that I don't have any feelings for him anymore," I explained.

"Do I need to call up Susan and get her to come over and talk some sense into you?" Tracey asked. Susan was the only other person who knew the details of that day as well.

"No, you don't need to throw threats around! Jude came into that room to tell me that he couldn't settle for being second best. He finally admitted to himself that my heart still belonged to another. I would have walked down that aisle if he didn't come to the room, you know that Tracey. I think he just finally realized what I could never tell him. I loved him, but not enough. I tried Tracey, I really did. I tried to let go of my first love; I was determined to be happy with Jude. But I had to be honest when he asked me. That was the hardest thing I had ever done... to be completely honest with him. He wanted my whole heart. Since I couldn't give it to him, I ended up breaking his heart.

"Whatever happened to the happy ever after? I know in my heart that I did the right thing. But by doing that, I gave up my dreams and desires. So when is it my time Tracey?" I begin to cry. "When will God fulfill my one desire? Or haven't I been punished enough for letting the one guy that was meant for me walk away when I was young and foolish? What, am I not good enough for God yet? Or does He have some big purpose for me living the single life, 'cause if He does, then I wish He would help me to get rid of the dream I have in my heart. Otherwise, it's not fair," I cried out.

This was the first time I had verbally voiced my feelings to someone other than the walls of this room about this.

Deep in my heart I feel not only hurt but also betrayed by God. This isn't something that I am willing to confess on a regular basis. As a Christian, who can honestly say that God has betrayed them? That just isn't right. And I know deep down it isn't true. "My ways are not your ways, nor are my thoughts your thoughts," the Bible says. I was in love once. I never really fell out of it. I was just too immature to realize what I had. I thought that marriage meant having to sacrifice too much. I wasn't ready for that yet. I was only twenty; I believed I had all the time in the world. Plus, I thought that if the love that we shared was real, then it would always be there. So I tried to test that theory. And was proved wrong. He walked away, and I let him go.

A few years later I met Jude. He swept me off my feet and made me laugh. He accepted me for who I was and gave me the courage to dare to dream. We dated for a bit before Jude confessed his love to me and asked me to marry him. I thought I had learned my lesson from last time, and I was determined not to let this dream pass away from me again. Even though there was always something between us, a part of me that I could never give him, he was willing to take me as I was. We had talks about settling for second best—but Jude was adamant that he was willing to take whatever I had to give him. So we planned our wedding. Jude is such a romantic that he wanted to be involved in every minute decision. The wedding was as much created by him as it was by me.

The night before our wedding, Jude came over to my apartment. He found me sobbing into my pillow. That was such a heartbreaking night for us. I felt that I was giving up the dream I had always kept hidden deep in my heart. I was marrying Jude out of fear—fear that if I didn't marry him, I would never find love again. Fear that I would lose everything. Jude was so gentle with me, so caring and loving. But I guess it finally dawned on him that what we had wasn't enough. There was more out there, and we were missing it. When he ended up walking into the chamber in the church where I was waiting, I knew that it was over. He had a desperate look in his eyes. All he asked of me was to be honest with him. He asked me one question. I think he already knew the answer to that question though, even before he asked it of me.

"Will you ever be able to give me your whole heart?"

That has to have been the hardest question I have ever had to answer. I couldn't lie to him, he deserved more than that. But I knew my answer would break his heart.

"I really don't know," was the only answer I could give him. I prayed that I would, I so desperately wanted to be able to give him my whole heart. But there was a deep part of me that knew; I just knew that I would never ever be able to say yes.

With a look of resignation, Jude slowly walked towards me. He took both my hands into his and pulled me into a hug. There was a note of finality in that embrace. With a kiss on the top of my head, and a touch of caress on my face, Jude whispered the words I will never forget.

"I can never be second best. I love you. But not enough to settle for only half your heart."

With that, he let go of me and turned around and walked out. He left by the back door, and in the background I could hear his car start up and drive away.

I stood there in stunned silence. I could feel the tears escaping from my eyes. I could hear a sob being torn from my throat. And then I collapsed.

And that is how I was found. Susan and Tracey came around me and hugged me. My father walked in, took one look at me and then after a glance out the window he left the room.

ONCE UPON A DREAM

My mother walked in and started to cry, demanding to know what had happened. Susan and Tracey gently escorted me out of the room, through the very door that Jude had left through and into the van that had brought me to the church. I later found out that it was my dad who announced that there would be no wedding. Both my parents and Jude's parents arranged to have all the catered food be given to the local woman's shelter and to the youth drop-in center. Everyone wanted to know what had happened. They started to blame Jude for walking out on me and breaking my heart. After days of walking in a daze, I felt strong enough to confess to Susan and Tracey what had really occurred. One week after that fateful day, Jude called me to see if I was ok. He apologized for leaving me to clear up all the mess. We both agreed that it would be best not to say anything to anyone, other than that it was a mutual decision on both parts not to get married. I doubt very much that it was enough to stop all the gossip and speculation, but at that point I really didn't care.

We have managed through the years to keep in touch. After a bit of a setback, our friendship resumed, and we've been able to regain normal lives once again. Once in a while we would talk about what had happened, but that was normally a topic that was better left alone. I haven't seen him in three years though, since that day that he walked out of the church. I always wondered deep down what would happen if he ever did come back. I guess now I know. It's not that I still love him, or that I want him back. I think what is hitting me the most is that once again my dream doesn't become true, while someone else's does. Purely selfish reasons.

"I don't know Wynne," replied Tracey as she just let me cry and bare my heart, "Scripture tells us that God grants us the desires of our heart. I don't want to spiritualize what you are feeling, hun, but when was the last time you really surrendered your desires to God's will?" Tracey asked me.

"Surrender? How many times do I need to surrender Tracey? Sometimes it feels like that is all I do! When am I allowed to say enough is enough, and ask when is it my turn for some happiness? I'm the only single one left of our group. Do you know what it's like to go to bed lonely every night? To not have that special someone there to talk to? Marriage and

children are my heart's desire. How can that not be God's will?"
I asked. Deep in my heart, I already know the answers. But it's
nice to vocalize my feelings for once.

"Marriage is a lot of hard work Wynne. You want to make
sure you're married to someone who can go through those hard
times with you," replied Tracey with a bit of a far-off look in her
eyes.

"Wynne, I know you are a strong person. Instead of
settling for second best, you have waited. Sometimes I wish…
well, let's just say not everyone has the strength to do that.
When Mr. Right does come along, you'll be able to offer so
much more into your marriage, Wynne, then if you had just
jumped the boat and married the first guy who came along.
Sometimes I envy you. You have been able to do things with
your life that I can't do because I have a family now. You quit
your boring, routine job; you took a huge step by opening your
own store and it's a success! You bought this home and made it
into your dream home. You are able to focus your love and
attention on your walk with God, and not worry about a lot of
little distractions. Don't beat yourself up because you're still
single. Enjoy it while you can!" Tracey finished by saying the
following in a soft whisper.

"Sometimes I wish I were still single."

Those little words just about broke my heart. I leaned over
and gathered her in my arms. It was my turn now to give her
the shoulder she needed and let her cry.

"You don't regret marrying Mike, do you?" I hesitantly
asked her.

She leaned back and took a deep breath.

"Sometimes," Tracey whispered. "Is that so horrible of
me?" she asked.

How do I answer this? Part of me is shouting "Yes, of
course it's horrible of you! Don't you realize the gift you have?
And what about those precious children of yours?" But instead
I keep quiet and just give her a small smile.

"I knew something was wrong, but I didn't realize it was
this bad. Gee Tracey, I'm so sorry! Are you guys just hitting a
bump in the road maybe?" I suggested. Who am I to really talk,
though, right?

"A bump, Wynne? More like a series of bumps. They just keep getting bigger and bigger. I know there has to be an end in sight, but I don't see a promising one anytime soon. The only end I see leads to a lot of hurt and pain." Tracey gives a big sigh.

"Oh Tracey." I replied. "I'm so sorry! Have you been able to talk to anyone about this? Are you guys going to be ok?" I asked. I honestly don't know what to say to her. I don't want to imagine that things are as bad as she is making it sound, but yet I don't want to trivialize her feelings either.

"Right now, Wynne, I honestly can't say. We'll get through. But whether it's together or apart, I honestly don't know," Tracey answered with a shake of her head.

"Now, enough about me. It's late and I do need to get home. But… I am going to find time to get away tomorrow, and I'll drag Susan with me. We'll come for coffee to Chocolate Blessings and we'll brainstorm about this party you are so determined to throw. I still don't know why you offered to do this—but since you won't back down, you're going to need all the support you can get!"

So with that being said, I walked her to the front door and gave her a big hug. We both needed it.

Walking to my bedroom, suddenly feeling rather lonely, I made a decision.

I'm going to get a cat!

If you get melted chocolate
on your hand, you're eating
it too slowly.

Chapter 6

I GOT MY CAT... well, kitten. Actually, to be honest, I am the proud owner of two kittens. I'm a sucker for punishment, but I couldn't just take one and leave the other behind. After calling the local animal shelter this morning before I went into the store, I found out that they had just received two kittens earlier this month. Today was the first day that they were offering them for adoption. The animal shelter found these kitties tied up in a bag, and they desperately needed some love and care. When I first saw them, my heart just broke. They looked so sad, lying beside each other. Their heads rested on their paws. As I was watching, one kitten began to play with the other. I think they were trying to put on a show for me... so that I would feel the necessity to take both. After hearing how they were found, I just couldn't leave one behind. So now I have the joy of taking care of two kittens, training them and making sure they behave themselves.

In the shelter they seemed too tame for their age. I was able to place them both in one carrier complete with a soft blanket for them to lie on. Since they seemed so well behaved I decided to take them into the store with me. I figured I could just leave them in the carrier in my office while I had to work out front. The worker at the shelter told me that with them being young and uncared for, I might find that all they do is sleep for the first day or so. Let me tell you—was she ever wrong!

When I walked into the store, Susan was waiting for me. It was her morning to open, which left me time to get any little running around that I need to do done. When she saw the carrier she immediately came over and peered inside to see what I had.

"Kittens! Oh, aren't they adorable! Wynne... you never told me you were getting kittens! Awww, look at them! Oh

Wynne, can I hold them? Pretty please?" she begged as she was already opening the door to the carrier.

"Isn't she just the sweetest thing? Oh, look at her cute little tongue, tiny little nose, and she's so soft! What's your name sweetie pie? Hmmm, little cupcake, what does ole Wynnie here call you?" Susan cooed at the kitten she was holding in her arms. I placed the carrier down and gathered the other kitten into my arms. I decided to let the 'ole Wynnie' comment pass for now.

"I think I'll call this one Jewel, and the one you have... Hmmm, I'm not sure yet." I said to her as I was stroking the kitten's fur. She has an amazing color, black and gold are mixed all throughout the fur. Right around her collar she has a ring of the gold coloring... reminding me of a necklace. I think Jewel will fit her perfectly.

"Oh Wynne, I think you should name this one Cocoa. Look at her coloring... almost like a chocolate brown, the color of frosting on a cake. So soft and sweet!" she tells me as she holds the kitten up to her cheek and rubs the fur across her face.

I think Cocoa is an excellent name for her, and in all honesty, how could I not have a cat named Cocoa?

Cocoa begins to lick Susan's face, which causes giggles to erupt from Susan. I take it she's a bit ticklish. After a few more cuddles with the kitten in her hand, Susan places Cocoa back into the carrier and then reaches for Jewel to hold as well. After the same routine, holding, cuddling, face tickling and giggles, Susan is ready to get back to work. I take the kittens and their carrier into my office in the back and gently tell them to go to sleep. I'm trusting that they will listen and obey me; after all, I am their new owner.

I walk out to the front to grab a cup of coffee when Susan barricades me into the corner of the store, behind the counter.

"Wynne Taylor, what is this news that Tracey told me about this morning? Why didn't you call me last night? I would have come over you know. Whatever possessed him to come over to your home unannounced and just dump on you with this news? He has no right to do that! And what possessed you, little missy, to offer to throw him, of all people, an engagement party?!" The words come exploding out of Susan's mouth. She is standing in front of me with her hands on her hips while she says this to me.

I had to laugh at her a little bit. I've had all night and morning to process this news, which she just recently found out.

"Don't you dare laugh at me, missy! I'm not the one making nonsense-type decisions here! Seriously!" she states as she roles her eyes and gives her head a little shake.

I take it she's not all that happy with me.

I'm not all that happy with myself either. But it's not like I can back out of this. I made a rash emotional decision, and now I need help to deal with the mess.

"Ok, ok...I admit I made the decision based on sheer emotion, and yes, I should have called you... but... you still love me. Now, let me by, so I can grab my coffee and then you can proceed to help me get out of this big mess," I admitted to her, while gently nudging her out of my way. With the way things are looking right now I am definitely going to need that coffee!

As I move away from the door, I can hear some gentle noise coming from my office. Ahh, the sounds of two kittens meowing! I smile softly as I head to the coffee counter. I can't wait to take them home! I'll need to make a list of things to get. Thank goodness the Dollar Store is nearby. I can grab some cat toys there, as well as some collars and dishes for food and water. Maybe I'll get them their own beds, or maybe one big bed for both of them to sleep in. I don't want them to get in the habit of sleeping with me in my bed.

Armed with coffee and some little treats, I head to the corner table where Tracey and Susan are huddled together with their heads joined, deep in conversation.

"I come bearing gifts," I stated with a bow.

"You've come to try to sweeten us up, more like it," replied Susan with a sarcastic tone to her voice. She knows me so well.

"Will it help?" I ask sweetly. I make sure I give my sweet little innocent smile, while I bat my eyelashes at the two.

"If it's chocolate, who cares?" came Tracey's remark as she grabbed the plate of goodies out of my hand.

"So," Tracey began as she immediately took a bite out of a chocolate macaroon the size of small child's hand. "Susan and I have decided that this needs to be a spectacular party, one that will take everyone's mind off the fact it's you throwing it. In fact, we'll spread it around that it's the group of us doing it, as old friends of Jude. We'll take the focus completely off of you as the hostess," she finished as she took another bite out of the macaroon.

"So you think that will work?" I asked a bit skeptically.

"No, I don't think it will work, but at least we're trying," Susan retorted back. I think I might have insulted her by being skeptical.

"And I do appreciate it! What would I do without you two to help me fix my messes? You know I love you... enough to share my chocolate with you, and that's a big deal!" It's a bit cheeky of a reply, but I need to get back into the good graces of Susan, and I figure a bit of teasing might help.

I glanced at Susan to see if it was working, and found her watching me with a thoughtful gleam in her eye.

"What?" I asked her.

"Have you had any more of your mystery man dreams?" she asked me back.

"Why?" I asked her hesitantly.

"What does that have to do with throwing this engagement party?" bewildered, Tracey asked Susan.

"It doesn't really have anything to do with the party per se, but I'm wondering if she offered to throw this party with a bit of desperation," she answered, still with that thoughtful look in her eye.

"I don't understand," replied Tracey. "How would desperation make her do this?"

"Well, the more she has these dreams, the more frustrated I've noticed her become, especially in regards to being single. I think that instead of being ready to deal with these issues she has, she just blurted out that she would throw this party, thus making sure that there was something else in her life that would take the focus off her real heart issue," Susan explained.

"Whoa, hold on a minute guys. I'm sitting right here. Don't you think you could at least try to notice me?" I asked with just a bit of frustration to my voice. I don't like being ignored. Nor do I like the fact that Susan is hitting awfully close to home right now.

"Only if you'll admit that I'm right," Susan shot back at me.

"Why do I have to admit that? So you can psychoanalyze me even more? No. Let's just drop this subject and deal with the issue at hand. Please?" I ask, addressing this question to both gals.

"Well, there's no reason to get your jimmies all in a knot," Tracey shot back at me. "Besides, you haven't answered the original question."

"What question?" I asked. "The one about whether or not I've had more dreams?" I answered. I'm not really sure I'm liking how this conversation is going right now.

"Yes, that question," Susan replied with a sigh.

I took my cup of coffee in both hands and brought it to my face. I inhaled slowly, absorbing the aroma within my senses. There's nothing like having the aroma of coffee surround you. I take a couple sips, trying to waste time before having to answer. Fortified with coffee, I finally respond.

"Yes, I had a dream last night. We were sitting by a pond. There was a pink blanket on the grass, and he had a beautiful hatbox sitting in his hands. It was gold with a pink ribbon. He was handing me the box, but I was hesitant to take it. I felt a bit afraid, but I took it in my hands and slowly began to undo the ribbon. I didn't open the box though. I think if I had, all the mysteries of my dreams would be answered, and I wasn't ready for that." I twirled my coffee cup on my hand while I described to them my dream from last night.

"Wouldn't you like to know who he is?" asked Tracey.

"Why? Susan already thinks I know who he is, but am just not willing to admit it!" I answered her back.

"True," Susan answered. "Have you thought any more about trying to find him?"

"Who? Trying to find whom? Ok, guys, I'm a bit lost here!" Tracey butts in before I have a chance to answer.

"Susan seems to think that I'm dreaming of Rich. I think she's wrong. Susan's convinced that if I only try to find Rich and get in touch with him, it might solve all my single problems. But I think he's married... after all, I heard he was getting married. So if I do try to get in touch with him I'll probably end up talking with his wife, and then how do I explain?" was my answer to Tracey. Evidently I haven't kept her abreast of this.

"And what if you find out that you're wrong? What then, Wynne?" Susan asked me. "What if he's been single all along, and it's just your stubbornness that has been keeping you apart? What will it hurt?" she asked me.

"It could hurt my heart. And that's not a risk I'm willing to take, Sue," I answered.

"TIME OUT," voiced Tracey in a rather loud and forceful voice. Both Susan and I glanced at her and found her to be leaning on top of the table looking at us rather sternly.

"Yes'm," I say meekly, while kicking Susan under the table.

"Alright. I can tell this is a somewhat sticky topic between the two of you, and obviously it is not going to be dealt with today. So can we please deal with the topic on hand... we have a party to plan!" Tracey lectures us in her 'don't give me any nonsense' mom tone.

While she is forcing us to calm down, I can hear a slight commotion in the background. I glance at Lily to see if she knows what is going on, but she is looking at me with a worried expression on her face. She's gesturing toward my office. What could possibly be making that noise in my office? The kittens are in their crate, and besides, I was told all they would do is sleep today. What could they possibly do?

I quickly get up and start to walk towards my office. That's when I begin to hear more noise. I hear something breaking, almost like glass. I walk faster. There is a louder noise, more distinguishable now... a loud meow or two. Oh boy. I did leave them in their crate, didn't I?

"Did you lock the crate gate?" Susan asked me as she followed me to the door.

"I think so," I replied as I opened the door cautiously. I begin to peer around the door, amazed at what I see. As I'm standing there in shock, out darts one of the kittens. Before I can react it is past me. The other one almost made it as well, but Susan grabbed a hold of it as it whizzed by me.

Behind me I can hear Tracey and Lily calling for the kitten. I have no idea where it has gone to, but I'll let them deal with it for now. Right now I have to face the mess in my office.

The site that greets me as I open the door is definitely one that will stay in my memory forever. If I had time to scrapbook, this is a sight that I would have taken a picture of. I have a thought in my head for a caption, but it's not one that should be spoken out loud!

The glass sound that I heard was of my lamp being knocked over and crashing to the ground. Any papers that were on my desk have mysteriously disappeared and somehow ended up all over my floor. My seat cushion, the one I lovingly toiled over to make, is now in shreds. My bottle of water is all over my desk—obviously I had forgotten to snap on the lid when I last used it. The dish of little candies that I like to keep on my desk is scattered about, the dish is on the floor unbroken, but the candies are everywhere. Ribbon that had originally been rolled up is now unrolled, and I'm not sure if the little puddles of water on my floor are actually water or something else unmentionable. What happened to my sweet little kittens that were supposed to sleep all day?

Susan glances around me and begins to giggle. I turn to look at her and give her one of those 'you've got to be kidding me' type of looks. She just keeps on giggling. It's hard to stay stern when she giggles, so I find myself beginning to smile. I try to keep it in, but it's so hard to do that eventually I find myself giggling as well. There's nothing like two girls giggling to attract attention. Up walks Tracey, holding the other kitten in her arms. She looks inside the office, gasps and then the tell-tale signs of a smile begin to show on her face as well. Soon all three of us are giggling. I leave Susan and Tracey holding the offending criminals while I walk inside to look for evidence of the crate being left unlocked. Amazingly, I find it unlatched. I look at Susan accusingly, but she just shrugs her shoulders, unable to speak due to her giggling. Tracey then looks at me, and points. I'm standing in a wet puddle. I groan. They giggle even harder. The kittens are wiggling in their captors' hands, trying to get free. I grab each offender and then place them together in the crate, ensuring I lock it soundly this time. They are making sure I hear their outrage in tiny little meows, but at this point I'm mute to their cries. My sanctuary has been destroyed, and my designer shoe is wet with what I really don't want to guess at, and my friends are just standing there giggling. This is now officially a crisis. I definitely need more coffee and chocolate!

With my office cleaned up and the supposedly "angelic" kittens finally sleeping, I find myself back at the table trying to make plans for the engagement party I mistakenly offered to throw. Armed with enough chocolate to satisfy any pre-menopausal woman we get down to business.

We finally come to the conclusion that we will hold the party in our church basement. Tracey loves to make homemade cards, so she will create invitations to the party. Susan will create her delicious masterpieces—desserts only, and I will be in charge of the decorating. Now this will be fun! I'll have to find out what types of things Stacey likes so I can turn our versatile basement into a beautiful room. In my head I have visions of pink lace, tulle and ribbon all over the place! Not a pretty vision. I'm hoping she will like soft colors, but not too girly. After all, this isn't just for the bride to be. Perhaps some heavy cream-colored tablecloths with classic black napkins will work. For the centerpieces we can fill assorted vases with water and clear cellophane wrapping paper, and sprinkle some pink sparkles throughout the water. I'll place a floater candle on top of the vases and add some tea light candles around each vase. Not too girly, nor too masculine. Simple, but elegant. Oh, and also some Gerbera flowers all over the room as well. Since it's winter, I might have to buy fake ones, but if they are nice enough, no one will mind.

With these thoughts racing through my head, I catch a glimmer of what I would like my engagement party to look like. I allow the thought that I am doing this more for me than for Stacey and Jude to linger for just a second before I toss the idea out and stubbornly announce to myself that this has nothing to do with me personally. With that in mind I take a walk through my store, dusting this, touching that, doing anything I can to take my mind off my reasoning for doing this party.

Things are a bit slow today in the store, so while Lily closes up, I'll take my kittens home and introduce them to their new place. I can hear them meowing in my office; they are probably ready to get out of their carrier and run free. If this afternoon was any indication as to how my life as a new pet owner will be like, I don't think I'll have a quiet evening for a while. What I was thinking when I decided to get both kittens, I have no idea!

LOVE
is a substitute for
CHOCOLATE.

Chapter 7

AFTER AN EVENING OF DE-CLUTTERING and kitty-proofing my home, I decided to spend some quiet time going through some old bridal magazines to try to get ideas of what we can do for Jude and Stacey's party. I used to hide my magazines from any guests that came through my door until I realized that it is quite normal for single women to have any number of bridal magazines scattered throughout their homes, with sticky notes protruding out of various pages within each magazine. It might actually be considered quite odd if you didn't find at least one or two of these magazines in any given single woman's home. After all, let's be honest. No matter our age, wedding-filled dreams are a part of who we are. Every woman knows exactly what they want their wedding dress to look like, they have already picked out their music, the song they will walk down the aisle to and who will be in their wedding party. For some, the invitations have already been chosen; they are just waiting for the groom's name to appear on them. Some might call them fantasy dreams, but for those of us who are living this fantasy life, it's our dream that will one day become a reality.

While reading "21 Ways to Fool Proof Your Wedding," and "How to Create the Wedding of Your Dreams, Not Your Mother's," my phone rings. Not only does this startle me, as I was deeply engrossed within these articles, but it startled Cocoa and Jewel, who had finally fallen asleep after a bout of playtime with my afghan. In the midst of me trying to reach the phone, while not loosing my page and trying not to get scratched by the frightened kittens, I manage to spill the hot coffee that I have resting on the edge of my armrest. I answer the phone with a "hot, hot, hot—ouch," and hear my mother's voice protruding through the line.

"Wynne, are you ok? What happened? Is this a bad time?"

81

"No, no, it's a fine time Mother," I answered while skipping around the floor trying to untangle myself from the afghan I somehow got caught up in. While trying to avoid the ever-growing puddle of coffee that is beginning to surround my feet, I notice out of the corner of my eye the kittens running through the doorway heading to who knows where.

"Well you don't sound fine. What happened this time?" my mom asked with a hint of disbelief in her voice.

"What do you mean by 'this time'? It's not like things happen to me a lot Mom. I just spilt some coffee on myself while trying to reach the phone," I answered in annoyance. The way my mom talks you would think I was a walking klutz.

"Wynne, don't take that tone with me! The last time I talked with you, your nose was bleeding because you fell out of bed. And before that you twisted your ankle while wearing your new dress shoes. Or what about the time you got that huge bump on your forehead by walking into a post while talking on your cell phone? Sometimes I think your head is up in 'la-la land!'" she exclaimed while listing all my most recent mishaps.

"Alright, already! How are you doing, Mom?" I asked.

"I'm fine—I'm calling to ask if you're feeling ok?" she asked me.

"I'm feeling fine mom. Why? What's up?" I'm beginning to get a little puzzled.

"What do you mean what's up? I just received a call from Jude's mother. That's what's up. She wanted to let me know what a nice daughter I have and how sweet and how kind it is of you to throw Jude and his fiancé an engagement party. An engagement party, Wynne! Do you know how stupefied I felt? I had no idea that he was engaged, let alone that you of all people would throw him a party to celebrate it! What made you do that, and why didn't you tell me?" It's amazing how mothers can sound both exasperated and astonished at the same time. It must be a gift they acquire.

"I just found out as well that he was engaged, and I was so shocked that I just blurted it out. I couldn't very well take it back. Besides, I'm actually looking forward to doing it now. You know how much I love to throw parties. Tracey and Susan are helping me, and we're making a joint effort, so that it won't appear that I'm the one throwing it," I tried to explain to her.

My mom has a tendency to enjoy being in the middle of all the fluff when something big is going on. If I can show that this isn't just me doing this, maybe she'll calm down.

"Well of course it will appear you are the one throwing it! Do you think no one will know? Nancy is practically bragging about it! As far as she is concerned, it's only right that the girl who broke her son's heart throw this party! Don't you care how this will look? Everyone will feel sorry for you... the girl who got left behind," Mom explained with a tone of pity in her voice.

I decide I had better sit down. This doesn't appear to be a short conversation. Better yet, I may as well get myself another cup of coffee. I'll need the fortification from it!

"Now, I've been thinking, Wynne." Oh-oh. Definitely not a good sign when I hear this coming from her lips. "What we need to do is get you a date for this party. That way no one will think you're still brokenhearted over losing Jude. It'll show that you have moved on with your life," she said proudly.

"And where do you propose I find this mystery man, oh Mother dearest?" I ask a bit sarcastically. As if I can just create a man from my dreams and make him pop out of nowhere. We live in a small town. You would think that if there were any available men in this town, I would have noticed them already.

"Well," she said a bit hesitantly, "how about you just leave that up to me?"

I laughed.

"Seriously, Wynne! You just concentrate on the party, and I'll find a date for you! No, no, don't worry; I already have the perfect gentleman in mind! He's handsome, Christian and very sensitive. He'll be just perfect for you. I think it's a wonderful idea!" she gushingly exclaimed while I continued to laugh.

What could it hurt? I've already done enough damage to my image as far as my friends are concerned. So what harm will bringing a blind date to an engagement party be? If it's so obvious that I'm the one who's throwing this party, then it will be just as obvious that I'm desperate enough to need to bring a blind date to it.

"Sure, Mom. You go ahead. Just make sure he's nice, ok, and that he knows this is for one night only! Nothing else, ok, Mom? Promise?" I replied.

"Really! You'll let me bring someone? Sure honey, no promises! Gotcha! Ok. Well, you have a good night now, I'll talk to you later!" and with that she hung up. She probably wanted to end this conversation before I had the chance to change my mind. I don't blame her. Smart move on her part!

Before I let my mind dwell on what I just agreed to do, I decide to drink my coffee and get back to my magazine. Hopefully when I wake up tomorrow, this will all have been part of a weird coffee-induced dream!

Is chocolate
the dream
or the reality?

Chapter 8

I'M HAPPY. MY FEET ARE WET, my jeans are sticking to my legs, but I feel happy. I can hear the waves, the soft gentle sound ringing in my ears. The sun is setting, vibrant shades of orange and reds. What's the saying? 'Red in the morning, sailors warning; red at night, sailors delight.' I feel at peace, all is right within my world. I look down and realize that there are a pair of arms surrounding my waist, tightly holding on to me. I feel the warmth of a body behind me, some hair tickling my neck at the back. I hear a deep sigh—was that me? I lean back and feel... loved. I'm happy, at peace and feeling loved. I'm facing the lake, with the waves gently crashing onto my feet. There are sailboats in the distance, bobbing up and down in tune to the rise and fall of the waves. I begin to imagine myself on that boat. How peaceful that would be.

With that one thought, I find myself on that very boat. My feet are no longer wet; in fact, I have designer sandals on with a summer dress swirling around my ankles. There's a gentle breeze that is lifting my hair off my neck and gently caressing me. It kind of tickles. I look around and all I see is water. It is even more peaceful than I thought. I hear footsteps walk across the deck, feel arms come around me, and see wine glasses in each hand. I take one; bring it to my nose, and smell. It's a sweet smell, like apple juice. I take a sip of the apple juice, letting the sensation of the sweet and bitter taste fill my mouth. I lean my head back, and hear a voice whisper in my ears, "I love you." Tingly sensations begin to sweep over me in waves. The three most romantic words that my soul has longed to hear. I close my eyes and hold those words deep into my heart. I love you, I love you, I love you. I can hear that deep voice huskily repeating those words to me. A soft whisper in my ear, spoken with hidden promises of lasting love, honor and commitment. An eternal love. An eternal promise.

I roll my head to the side. I'm wanting to turn around, to whisper those secrets that are hidden deep within my very being. I feel the soft caress of the wind against my neck. It begins to tickle. I bring my hand up to rub that very spot when I feel my finger being bitten. Bitten? Ouch—that hurt!

I quickly rise from my slouched position on the couch and hold my finger. There are little tiny bite marks. That wasn't the wind caressing my neck; it was a little kitten licking me. I put my hand to my neck and it's wet. Those weren't gentle kisses from my dream man. They were little kitten kisses. So much for my romantic dream! I scoop up the kitten responsible for waking me from my dream and cuddle it against my cheek. If I close my eyes, I can almost hear the soft soothing sound of the waves while they wash upon the sand, I can almost feel those warm arms holding me close, and I can almost recapture that feeling of timeless love. Almost. I can feel the sensations begin to slip away. Who is this mystery man? Could it be Rich, as Susan believes? What if it was him? Why can't I let this go, why do I continually hold onto that dream in my heart of my first love? Grow up, Wynne. Time to move on. Yet, what would it hurt to perhaps do a quick little search on the Internet as Susan keeps encouraging me to do? Unless he was important or something, I doubt very much I would find anything on him. Yet, what would it hurt? No one would need to know. And if I don't find anything, then I can tell Susan, and that will be the end of it all. And if I do find something? Well, I doubt that will happen.

I look at the clock. It's only a little after 10 pm. Just enough time to do a quick search, check my email and head off to bed. I could use another cup of coffee, but since I'm fresh out of decaf, I'll have to enjoy a nice cup of hot chocolate. While the kettle is going, I route through my fridge to see if I have any whipping cream left over. There's nothing like a cup of hot chocolate with whipped cream on top! Well, if it has chocolate shavings, it might be a little bit better, but it's late, and I don't want to take the time to make some fresh shavings. Mental note to self: make a fresh batch of shavings tomorrow.

Armed with a large cup of hot chocolate, I settle back on my couch, move the kittens to the other side and place my laptop on my knees. I make sure my hot chocolate is safely sitting on my side table, and that the kittens are safely on the other side of the couch before I log into the Internet. Bypassing my email for the moment, since, after all, this quest won't take much time, and if I get this out of the way, then it will be off my mind.

Where do I start? I bring up Google's home page and enter in Rich Carradine. Amazingly it turns out that there are over 70,000 different sites that have both the word Rich and Carradine in it. Like I'm going to search them all. Taking a quick glance at the first few pages was like taking a quick dip in a fantasy novel—instant and utter confusion. There has to be an easier way to find information on here! So I decide to type in the name of the university I last heard he taught at. Just as I'm about to hit Search, the phone rings.

Susan's perky voice is on the other line.

"Hey girly, it's not too late to call is it?" she asks with a slight laugh to her tone.

"No. It's only after 10 PM, and only the bored and married are in bed! What's up?" I responded with a bit of sarcasm. I can hear more muffled giggling from her, and I begin to feel a bit annoyed.

"Sorry," she answers back, still laughing, "I had a little bit too much chocolate and coffee tonight, and Matt wants to go to bed, so he suggested I bug you instead of him!" she explains in amongst her many giggling episodes. One thing I learned about Susan right from the start is that she is very sensitive to caffeine. Too much in her system and you can literally see her bouncing off the walls. It's a scary sight actually.

"Nice guy you have there! He's the one who married you, so why is it I'm the one stuck with you whenever he doesn't want to deal with you?" came the only response that I could think of. I made sure I laughed a little when I said it—did I mention that she is very sensitive emotionally when she's had too much caffeine as well?

"Because he knows how much you love me, and you're the only one besides him who will put up with me. Those were his exact words too!" she told me, albeit a little dramatically.

"So, what are you doing anyways?" she asked me.

I hesitated a little bit. Do I really tell her what I am doing? I can only imagine her response.

"Hmmm, I'm on the net. Nothing too important," I replied, a bit evasively.

"What do you mean, nothing important? Are you searching for more goodies for the store, or talking to your gal pals in one of you 'forums?'" she asked. She never takes my answers at face value, she always has to prod and find out the exact details.

"My gal pals are a good source of those so called goodies for our store you know!" I mumble a bit defensively to her.

This subject has been a source of contention in our friendship the past few years. I belong to a couple of online forums that pertain to various subjects, consisting mainly of crafts and Christian issues and weight loss. I have a few that I spend the majority of my time on. These 'groups' have become important to me. Although I have never seen these women face to face, I can honestly say that they have become deep sisters of my heart. I am able to share a part of me with these ladies that I normally feel I have to hide from others. This is what Susan has a problem with. She's not always the first person I go to for prayer or for advice. Depending on the situation or the time, I'll post a little message to the ladies requesting their prayers and their wisdom. Another group that I frequently visit is a craft forum, filled with talented ladies from all across the world. I have literally stocked Chocolate Blessings full of their handmade goodies. I firmly believe in supporting crafters who create things from their heart. I know how hard it is to start a business, and when you do it from home, using this money to help pay bills—any orders that they receive is a blessing.

"I know, I know; no need to get so defensive, Wynne. So is that what you are doing?" she persistently asked. Did I mention that she can also be quite stubborn when she wants to be?

"Umm, not quite. I'm just doing a little searching, wasting mindless brain cells searching for anything and everything that comes into my head. So... what about you? What did you do this evening that caused you to overload on caffeine?" I asked, hoping to change the subject.

"The chocolate and coffee, you mean? Oh, Tracey stopped by to chat. I was in the middle of trying out a new recipe, so of course we had to taste test it and nothing goes better with chocolate than coffee. I think between the two of us, we both drank a full pot! I should have made decaf!

And before you ask why I didn't call you, I tried but your phone was busy! Then one thing led to another, and Tracey just left a few moments ago. Don't worry, I saved you some of my experiment! It's quite good actually. If Matt can keep his hands off them, I'll bring some into the store tomorrow," Susan promised.

"Hmmm, it must be good if Matt likes it! What did you make? If it's chocolate, you know I'll like it!" I said to her. It wasn't fair of her to dangle a little piece of chocolate in front of my face and not tell me what she made!

"Oh, you'll like it alright! But you'll have to wait and see. It's a bit hard to explain. So... what were you searching for when I called? Something for your kittens, furniture for your home, a new recipe or maybe you took my advice and started to look for Rich?" she asked. She's like a hound dog that has caught a faint snip of a rabbit. Now she'll go rooting in every little hole, until she finds what she's looking for!

I stayed silent for a moment. I don't want to actually lie to her. But I'm not quite ready to admit that I gave in either.

"You did, didn't you! You did a search for Rich! I knew you would! So, what did you find? Come on, Wynne—don't get all quiet on me now!" She exclaimed with an eager tone to her voice.

I can just picture a wide smile on her face, and that "I knew it!" gleam in her eye. If she isn't sitting down, she's probably doing a little jig on her floor, and if she is sitting down, she most likely has one of her arms raised in victory!

"Alright, alright!" I sighed in resignation.

"Yes, I decided to do a quick search, just to satisfy you. And no, I didn't find anything. Are you happy now?" I asked her, admittedly with a bit of a snotty tone in my voice.

"Happy? Of course I'm happy! But you obviously haven't looked in the right places. How could you not find anything on him?" Susan asked.

"Did you look up his name? The school where he teaches? Did you try to find his phone number? Really, Wynne, did you look very hard, or have you just hardly looked?" she persisted in asking me.

"No, Susan. I just did a quick search of his name. Just before you called I thought of typing in the school's website, but do you know something I don't know? You certainly have a lot of suggestions as to where I should look. Maybe you've already done all the hard work—do you want to fill me in?" I asked her with a hint of accusation in my voice. I'm starting to feel slightly annoyed, and I'm really not sure why that is.

"You know what? I'm starting to not like your tone right now, Wynne. I think it's time I let you go. It's probably time I should go and head to bed anyways. Oh, I forgot to tell you. Your Latte Ladies group is meeting in the morning. I'll see you in the morning, ok?" With that being said, Susan hung up the phone.

Great. Now I've done it. She was probably just trying to offer suggestions, and here I go and bite her head off. Jesus, please forgive me! I'll apologize to her in the morning, and I promise to not be upset if she doesn't bring me any of her treats that she made tonight!

With those thoughts in mind, I actually find myself typing in the various suggestions that she made in searching for Rich. I type in the name of the school I last knew him to teach at. As I waited for the web page to load up, I began to feel a little queasy in my stomach. Thank goodness for high speed Internet! I click on the link to the Alumni page. As I scroll down, I really find myself a bit nervous. What if I do see his picture and description? Do I want to read it? What if he is married, how will I react? What if he's single? Is it right if I pray that he is still single or should I pray that he's married? What would I do anyways if I found he was still single? It's not like I could just call him up out of the blue and say, "Hey, I've been dreaming of you lately, and I think I'm still in love with you!" Could I really say that? I shake my head—of course I couldn't. Who in their right mind would start off a conversation like that?

Just before I decide I'm the world's biggest chicken ever and click off the site, I see his name. It basically jumped out at me. Take a deep breath, Wynne, breathe in and breathe out. I close my eyes, whether from my innate chicken personality or just for some added strength, I'm not sure which. I say a quick prayer, "God help me," and open my eyes.

There he is. As handsome as ever. With the same wavy hair and sparkling eyes he looks the same, only a bit older. Oh my—he still makes my stomach do those little fluttery dances, and my heart beats just a little bit faster. Looking through his bio beside his picture, it says nothing about his family. That could be a good thing, right? I quickly glance up to see if any other bios contain personal information and see several where they talk about the wives and children. Whew! So, maybe he still is single!

Then the thought actually hits me. He could still be single! I feel a huge smile begin, and I actually hear myself giggle. Me. Giggling. Getting up out of my chair, I do a little jig, hands raised, laughing. It's almost like some hope for the future has re-entered into my heart. I'm not sure what I will do with this, but in the meantime, I will just savor this new knowledge.

Deciding that I don't need to do any further searches, I shut down my computer, hold this new thought close to my heart, and head off to bed. Who knows, maybe my dreams will be different tonight. Maybe I'll see my true love's face!

Coffee & Chocolate—
women's best friends.

Chapter 9

I'M LATE. THERE'S NOTHING WORSE than being late with the Latte Ladies. The last time I was late there were no goodies left, and I was volunteered to work a craft table at the local Kids' Fair day. I didn't mind working at the Kids' Fair, but the fact they didn't leave me any goodies really hurt! I learnt that day that you never want to be late with the Latte Ladies.

There they all were, sitting at the corner table. I could see a basket in the middle. Must be Susan's treat that she made last night. Please don't let it be empty!

"Good morning, Wynne!" Lily greeted me from the counter as I stopped to pour myself a cup of coffee.

"Hi there Miss Lily! How are you doing this morning? I thought Susan was coming in to open up," I commented as I looked around to see if I could spot Susan.

"Oh, Susan did! But I knew you had your Latte Ladies this morning, so I thought I would come in just in case it was a bit busy. With this being the Christmas season, I just figured you deserved to actually sit down and enjoy your coffee rather than popping up here to help out with customers," Lily replied as she gave me a bit of a cheeky smile.

Ok, ok. I admit it. I'm a hands-on type of person, and I can't seem to sit still when the store is full of customers. If I'm not at the front counter ringing in their purchases, then I'm browsing throughout the store chatting with those who come in, offering suggestions, pouring coffee. I definitely have a people person character.

After quickly sticking my tongue out at Lily for her comment, I grab my coffee and a fresh muffin and head over to the table to join the ladies.

"Good morning there, ladies! Please tell me you were nice enough to save me a few goodies this morning!" I greeted them as I gave them all little hugs as I passed by them.

"You snooze, you lose! You should know that by now, Wynne," said Joan as she quickly placed her hand in the basket to grab one of the delicious treats.

"Awww, be nice, Joan! Wynne looks like she had a bit of a rough morning. Look, she's even wearing her shirt inside out this morning. I think she deserves one of those goodies!" Judy replied back as she gently patted my arm in sympathy. I quickly look down at my top and realized she was right. It is inside out!

"I didn't sleep well," I muttered quietly as I left the table feeling a bit flustered and entered into the washroom to change my shirt around. I can't believe I would actually walk out the front door like this!

As I walk out the bathroom door I hear some laughter coming from the table. Hoping that laughter isn't directed at me, I peek around the corner to see what is going on. Judy is leaning into the table with an intense look on her face. That can only mean one thing. She is telling one of her stories.

Judy McNeil is the mother of our group. I like to think of her as "old and wise" although she really isn't all that old. Judy has a whole passel of children—I think a total of six if I counted right last time. I'm not sure how she does it, to be honest, yet she never seems to be worn out. If Judy isn't at home with her family, you'll find her bringing some home-baked goodies to a lady in our church, volunteering at one of the many functions that always seem to be happening in our town, or joining us for our Latte Ladies. I remember her saying once that Latte Ladies is an outlet that is just for her, a venue that God uses to revitalize and bring some joy into her life. That caused me to really think about what Latte Ladies meant to me. It used to just be a Bible study that I went to once a week, until it was this very group of ladies that stood by me when my life seemed to be in shambles. I now thank God for them on a daily basis. He has used them to touch my life in so many different ways.

"Now, that looks better, Wynne," piped up a cheeky Joan as I sat down in my chair. "You must have had a rough night to not remember how to get dressed! Here, I saved you a goodie that Susan made. You will just love them! She calls them Turtle squares and they go perfect with a cup of coffee," chattered Joan as I reached into the basket with the hopes that someone at least saved me one treat.

"Thanks. Yes, I had a rough night, a rough morning, and I definitely need this right now! Nothing takes the blues away like chocolate in the morning!" I said just before I took a bite of the Turtle Square.

"Oh, get ready… here comes her reaction!" said Tracey.

"Hmmm, ohhhhh, hmmmm," I moaned as I took a bite of the delicious treat! I am known to savor chocolate. To take a bite of any type of chocolate, whether it's a cookie, square or even a chocolate bar, and not savor that first sweet taste as it melts on your mouth is definitely a sin in my books! There is a technique to this I have discovered. I've tried time and time again to explain this to the Latte Ladies, but they just don't appreciate a good thing when they bite into it!

First, you need to smell the chocolate. You can always get your taste buds going on hyper drive just by one smell. Can you smell the mint or caramel in what you are about to enjoy? Maybe it is hazelnut? You'll never know though until you smell it first. Then you need to close your eyes as you take that first bite. Gently sink your teeth into the soft chocolate, let it sit on your tongue for a few seconds, and savor the unique feeling of that chocolate beginning to melt on your tongue. Allow the sensation to sink in, and you'll begin to feel it all through your body. It begins as one of those "Ah" moments, and then you get that feeling that all is right with the world. When you have a piece of chocolate in your mouth, nothing else exists!

I always get teased by these ladies for how much I enjoy my chocolate. I've never hidden the fact that chocolate is one of my passions in life. I think that is why Chocolate Blessings is so successful. It's a full-blown passion for me. How many people can honestly say that they have taken their top passion in life and made it a success?

"Make fun of me all you want, Tracey, but you know that you love chocolate just as much as I do!" I said after I enjoyed my first bite.

"True, but no one else has made eating chocolate an art!" she retorted back at me.

"Ladies, ladies… enjoy your chocolate and call it even!" Pastor Joy said to us with a smile on her face.

"I think we might need to give Wynne an extra treat this morning. She's going to need it, I think," mentioned Judy as she patted my arm again.

"I'll take the chocolate, but why do you think I need it?" I asked. I'm beginning to feel a bit curious now.

"Well, dear," Judy began, "we heard about this party that you are throwing and we are all a bit concerned. Now don't get me wrong. We are here standing by you, and we will help you plan it, but we were there for you when he left. We're a bit concerned about how you are handling all this right now."

I look at the ladies with what I'm sure is coming across as an exasperated look.

"Tracey put you up to this, didn't she?" I asked. I smiled at them, perhaps trying to reassure them that I really am ok.

"No, hun." Pastor Judy said softly. "Jude's mother, Nancy, called me up yesterday to tell me. She assumed you would want to use the church basement to hold this party, and she wanted to make sure that it would be available," she explained.

I slumped in my chair at this news.

"Nancy called you? Oh dear. I can imagine what she had to say about this," I said as I sighed.

"Yes, she had a bit more to say, but that is neither here nor there. Wynne, what I'm concerned about is the fact that you offered to throw this party! You know you don't have to do this. I'm sure one of us, or any other lady is our church for that fact, would have offered to throw this party had we found out. Actually, I think Nancy would have loved to have thrown a huge shower for her son and his fiancé," Pastor Joy told me.

"In all honesty, it was spur of the moment decision. Jude stopped over one night unannounced and told me the news. I was a bit shocked and overreacted. Tracey came over for our girls' night and because I had been embarrassed as to how I reacted to his news, I just blurted out that I would throw the party," I admitted to the group.

"But, the more I think about it, the better it sounds to me. If I throw this party, then everyone will realize that I'm not pining over my ex fiancé and that I'm ok with him getting married. Everyone knows how much I love to throw parties, so no one should think twice about this. Right?" I asked, sincerely hoping for their agreement.

ONCE UPON A DREAM

There was a moment of silence around the table. I started to doubt that I would receive their agreement.

"Wynne, honey. Are you serious?" asked Joan.

"I thought I was," I answered a bit hesitantly. The way the ladies were looking at me began to cause a little bit of worry to seep into my mind.

"Wynne, we were there, remember? All the times you broke down sobbing because he up and left you at the church alone. We've been there when you have been angry with God because you thought He wasn't hearing your heart's cry. We heard you when you told us of your secret hope that if Jude was ever to come back to town you might get back together with him. Wynne, you can't fool us honey, no matter how hard you try." Judy spoke softly to me while she held my hand.

"I know. But obviously it's God's will for me to be alone right now. Otherwise Jude would have come back sooner and without a fiancé in tow. I have to accept that. I have to accept that there is a strong probability I will be single for the rest of my days. Just because I might not like the idea, doesn't mean I have to hide from it, though. Right?" I asked her. Why is it everyone seems committed to making me face my deep issues with this whole Jude/engagement party blow-up?

"Wynne, just because Jude obviously isn't the one for you doesn't mean that God wants you to be single for the rest of your life! Look at me, I didn't get married until I was *thirty-five*," Pastor Joy admitted. "God has just been preparing you, getting you ready so that when that perfect man does come along there will be nothing holding you back," she encouraged me... or tried to at least.

"Don't you think that by throwing this party, it shows that I have moved on with my life? I really don't think this is such a bad idea. It's just one friend throwing another friend an engagement party. What's so wrong with that?" I asked them with a hint of desperation to my voice.

Tracey hands me another chocolate turtle and pushes my coffee cup closer to my hands.

"There's nothing wrong with a mere friend throwing another friend a party. But when it's an ex fiancé throwing the party, then it looks like she is trying really hard to prove not only to herself, but also to the rest of the world that she has

101

really moved on with her life," responded Tracey. I give her points for at least trying to butter me up first with chocolate.

I took a deep sigh. I could never hide anything from these ladies, and I'm not even going to start trying now. I might as well admit the truth, open myself up completely, and trust that they will still love me enough in the end to help me plan this party.

"Ok. I admit that I have some issues. And I admit that offering to throw this party probably wasn't the best idea I've ever had. And I'll admit that I probably still have some feelings left for Jude. But, and this is a big but, I don't love him anymore nor am I jealous that he is getting married and I'm not," I exclaimed to the group.

They all looked at me with their eyebrows raised. I guess they don't believe me.

"Ok, ok. So I might be a little bit jealous that he's getting married. But only a little bit! What girl wouldn't be? But I made the choice not to marry him three years ago. If I'm still holding some unrealized feelings towards him, I have to let them go. I don't understand why he's getting married and I'm not. I don't understand why God is withholding that desire from me. It's like He keeps dangling that dream in front of me, and yanking it whenever I start to hope too much on it. That's not fair!" I cried out.

I definitely need more chocolate now! Seeing that the basket is now empty, I rise from my seat and hurry over to the counter to fill a plate full of muffins and cookies. I need something to take my mind off my emotions; otherwise I will start crying soon.

There is a nice lull at the table when I return with the plate of muffins. As everyone is helping themselves to the treats, I venture some quick peeks at all their faces. Some are looking back at me with speculation in their eyes; others are fixated solely on their muffin or cookie.

I take a deep breath. Perhaps I can steer the conversation away from my unsettled issues and onto the major issue at hand. The party.

"Admitting that there are still some issues that I obviously have to deal with is one thing. But actually having to plan this party is another. I need some help," I asked them.

Joan immediately rushed to my rescue. Bless her heart!

"Well, of course you need help, sweetie! That's why we are here. I've already made a list of the major tasks that need to be done. You just tell me what you have planned and we'll go from there."

So with the conversation successfully changing directions, we proceeded to spend the remaining hour left of our study making party plans. Once again, these ladies have saved the day!

"Hey, girl! Your sign says you're closed, so come with me!" I hear a familiar voice call out to me as the doorbells jingle their merry tune.

"Susan! What brings you by? You should be at home snuggled up to your hubby in front of your roaring fire." I smile at her while continuing to close up the store. The beginning of the day and the end of the day are two of my many favorite times. There's nothing satisfying like seeing empty shelves that need to be restocked, a cash register slightly fuller than normal, and knowing that baking needs to be done to fill the counter again. Well, that part isn't always my favorite, 'cause unless I can cajole Susan into baking, I have to come up with some pretty spectacular masterpieces.

"Matt is at a meeting tonight at the church. The men's group is having a 'chef contest' tonight. I made Matt take my apron and hat with him so that he looks like a real chef," she explained to me while she started to giggle.

"Which apron did you give him Sue?" I asked. "Your professional white one, or your girly pink one that I bought you for Christmas last year?"

"Well," she hesitates slightly, "I stuffed it all into a plastic bag, so he won't find out until he gets there—but of course the pink one!" Susan giggles.

I started to laugh! That was exactly something she would do! I can just see Matt's face now as he pulls out his chef's uniform in front of all those guys!

"Too bad you didn't have someone to take a picture," I said to her as I gathered up my coat and purse.

"Oh, but I do! I called Pastor Miles who is leading the group tonight. I told him what I did, and he can't wait to see Matt all dressed up! He's agreed to take a few pictures for me," she said as she grabbed my arm and led me to the front door.

"Now that's a sight I definitely wouldn't want to miss! So, where are we going?" I asked her as I locked up the door and started out towards her car.

"I thought we could go out for dinner tonight, just you and me! It's been awhile since we've gone out and had some girly fun. I'm in the mood for some nice Italian food, how does that sound?" she asked while doing a little dance in the snow by her car door.

"Well, you definitely seem to be in quite the mood tonight!" I said to her. "What's up? I didn't think we were doing the girly night thing until next week," I asked with a hint of hesitation to my voice.

Susan is normally a spontaneous type of girl, but she's acting a bit, hmm, I don't know, strange tonight. Something is definitely up.

"What do you mean, what's up? Why does something have to be up when all I want to do is go and have some fun girly time tonight? I don't want to wait until next week." She stopped her twirling and stood there with her hands on her hips, almost like she was ready to do battle.

I place my hands up in the air. "Alright, alright! I give up!" I say as I start to laugh. It feels good to laugh. I think I need this tonight.

"Good! Now get in the car and let's go! I'm hungry," Susan said to me with a sigh as she stepped into her car and started it up.

We ended up at Mama Rose's, the best little spot in town for Italian food. I absolutely love their Fettuccini Alfredo. I'm positive that their sauce is homemade. I usually try and do take-out here at least every week as a special treat to myself. Once in a while I'll come in and dine, but not too often. This place has a real romantic flavor to it, and it's too much to handle at times.

The moment we walk in we are instantly greeted by Mama Rose herself.

"Wynnie, Wynnie! So good to see you!" she greets me while enfolding me in a warm hug and kissing me on each cheek. "It's been too long since you came in here! I haven't seen you in over a week now. I made a cheesecake just for you, and you never come! Wynnie, Wynnie, what am I gonna do with you?" she says as she pats each cheek gently.

"Susan! Now this is a treat! So good to see you! I remember when you girls used to come in here all the time. Then you get married, and you don't come in as much! And where is that handsome man of yours?" she asks as she looks behind us.

"It's just us, Mama Rose! We're having a girls' night tonight," I say to her as she takes us to a secluded table.

"A girls' night! Just the thing you need I think! Now you come this way. Best spot in the room, nice corner where you girls can have a quiet evening. And I will have a mochachino with chocolate whip cream and shavings to you in a jiffy. Come, come!" Mama Rose clapped her hands while leading us to our table.

"Mochachino and cheesecake! Mama Rose, you spoil me!" I declared to her as I placed my arm around her thick waist and gave it a squeeze.

"Ah, Wynnie, you need to be spoilt every now and then!" she replied as a blush swept across her face.

"Now, sit, chat and enjoy!" and with that she left us and disappeared behind the counter to make our sweet drinks.

As we sit, I take a look around the restaurant. I absolutely love how Mama Rose has created the ambiance for the room. White Christmas lights are wrapped around the walls and create a soft glow throughout the room. Ivy is intertwined amongst the lights, and there are long wooden shelves along each wall holding antique items that range in size and detail. On one wall you can find white water pitchers set among antique-looking mirrors that are surrounded by either potted plants or flowers. There are wall sconces everywhere with dimmed lights to help create the soft atmosphere that is part of this place. Soft classical music is being played somewhere. You almost expect to see musicians suddenly appear walking among the tables, serenading each couple as they hold hands and gaze into each other's eyes. On each table is a cream-colored tablecloth, complete with a dazzling place setting and a candleholder. Each corner holds a tall plant, and there are mirrors situated in the perfect spots around the room to help catch the soft glow from the candles, and lights. It's the perfect setting for romance.

After a server brings our mochachinos, Susan and I settle in for a girl fest.

I'm feeling a bit leery of where our discussions might lead us. You never know with Susan what journey her thoughts will take you. I figured it might be safer if I was to start the journey before she actually did.

"Ok Sue, fess up. What do you have up your sleeve?" I asked her. With all her dancing, laughing and sly looks, I knew something was up.

"Well, why don't we just enjoy our chocolate drink, eat some good food, and then go from there?" Susan suggested while she toyed with the glass in her hand.

"I'm game," I told her, "as long as you promise to fess up later on! I'm not going to let you get out of whatever it is you have to say that easily!"

Susan just laughed at me as our server came to the table with complimentary garlic bread from Mama Rose. She even topped half of it with melted cheese. Yum, just the way I like it!

We both decided to order our usual. I had the fettuccini while Susan ordered the special three-cheese lasagna. If we work this right, we will sit here long enough to enjoy our food, chat up a storm with each other, and still leave room for dessert at the end. When Mama Rose makes one of her special cheesecakes, you are just not allowed to pass that up! I am really hoping that she made her special Turtles Cheesecake, or even a Chocolate Chip Cheesecake.

After chatting about normal girl things, from the likes of the new shoes Susan bought this week, to my need for new throw cushions on my couch (thanks to my new pets), Susan decided to drop a bomb on me.

"So, Wynne. I got a hold of Rich and found out he is still single." Boom!

I could hear the whistle of the bomb from the moment Susan began with 'so, Wynne.' When I heard the word 'Rich,' I knew it was directly above me, and when she said 'single,' that was when the bomb exploded. I felt paralyzed for a split second. Complete and utter shock and disbelief. Shock that this came out of nowhere. Disbelief that she would actually go behind my back and get in touch with Rich. I feel myself becoming immersed within these feelings until from the depths of my being I manage to resurface and actually hear what she just said.

"You did what?!" came exploding out of my mouth. The disbelief and the beginnings of what I can only describe as outrage could be heard within those three words.

Susan just sat there calmly, nibbling on a breadstick while I felt like I was inside an out-of-control locomotive.

"I found Rich for you," she said as she let another bomb drop and explode around me.

I couldn't believe I actually heard her say that!

"Why?" I asked her in stunned disbelief. "Why would you do that?"

"Wynne, one day you are going to wake up from your dreams and realize it is all too late. I don't want that to happen to you. I love you. I'm your best friend. Why wouldn't I do this?" she confessed to me while still sitting calmly eating her breadstick.

"Um, maybe because I never asked you to? Or how about because you knew that I wouldn't want you to? Really, Susan, I'm not all that happy about this. I can't believe you would go behind my back and do this!" I answered her in even more disbelief, if that was even possible.

"Ok. So, get over the shock, and realize what I originally said to you. Rich is still single. 100% free to take if you so desire! No, I didn't tell him that you are looking, or even dreaming. I just casually said hi to him and asked him what was new," Susan told me before she took another sip of her fresh hot mochachino.

"Oh, and by the way, he said to say hi," she added. It felt as if another bombshell just hit me.

He said to say hi. He actually thought of me, enough to say hi to me. I feel a smile start to take place—not on my face, 'cause there was no way I was going to let Susan off the hook that easily—but definitely in my heart.

"Oh, you just casually said hi to him. How casual, Susan? Did you meet him on the street, bump into him and then realize who he was? Where did you see him Susan? And why haven't you told me about this sooner?" I asked her. Something smells just a bit fishy here.

"Well, casual enough." Susan admits, albeit a little bit hesitantly. I knew it! I knew something wasn't right!

"No, don't look at me that way, Wynne! I received a letter in the mail from the University asking for donations. I noticed his name as a teacher there along with his email address. I just thought I would drop him a line and say hi. After all, we are old friends! I figured that if I could find out if he was still single or not, then I would know whether or not to encourage you to find him. You know he's the man in your dreams, Wynne. You can't deny that! You still love him, or at least hold on to the love you felt for him. What could it hurt to get in touch with him and see where it will lead? There's no 'significant' other in the picture, so what have you got to lose? And don't say your heart! I've heard that line one too many times lately. It won't work with me, Wynne," Susan lectured.

"I'm not giving you a line Susan. What if I'm not actually in love with the man, but rather with the idea of the man? In my dreams he might be Mr. Perfect, but in real life, he's probably far from it. My heart will get hurt, Susan. Hurt, because if it doesn't work out, then I have been living in fantasy land, being in love with the idea of a man," I confessed to her. I leaned forward onto the table and placed my head in my hands. It was hard to admit that to her.

Susan covered my hands with hers.

"Well of course you are in love with the idea, Wynne! But don't you think it's time that you get a hold of the man and get to know him? I doubt very much that it would take long for you to quickly fall in love with the actual man instead of the idea."

I raise my head and glance at Susan. She is giving me a sympathetic smile. She does understand what I am going through.

"I know you are right. But I am actually enjoying the idea. It's a lot safer!" I admitted to her.

Susan began to laugh. Mama Rose was walking through the dining room and quickly came over to our table. Mama Rose glanced from Susan to myself, shrugging her shoulders and sits down. There's nothing Mama Rose likes better than to be with a crowd that laughs.

"Oh, Mama Rose. Wynne is trying to make me believe that she is a chicken. Can you believe that?" Susan continues to chuckle while shaking her head.

I give her a glare, trying to silently portray that she needs to be silent. It's one thing to admit my weakness to my best friend. It's another to admit it to anyone else.

"Wynnie? The same girl who created a business out of nothing but sheer passion? Who was strong enough to hold her head high after being left at the altar? The same girl who isn't afraid to dine alone or to build her own dream home out of a run-down house? Not our Wynnie!" Mama Rose mockingly exclaimed while holding both hands to her chest.

Mama Rose can be too cute at times. Especially when she tries to be serious when you know inside she is really laughing.

"Enough already!" I exclaimed at them while giggling.

"Yes, that Wynnie," I said as I glanced at Mama Rose. "It's a whole lot easier to be strong in areas that don't affect the deep secrets in your heart!" I told them.

"Well of course it is, my girl. But who do you think gives you that strength for those areas? The same one who will expose those deep secrets so you can be a stronger person! There is no secret that is too deep for the light of God to penetrate and expose. He will only expose those secrets for your benefit, not for your harm or for your humiliation. Too many people see their weaknesses as a hindrance in their lives. Instead we need to see those very weaknesses as secret strengths. Imagine the things God can do through us when we surrender to him those areas that are the most protected," Mama Rose said softly to me while gently patting my hand.

I close my eyes. Lifting my head high, I try to force the tears that are threatening to escape to stay behind my eyelids. I'll just let them think I'm praying while I try to compose myself.

Sniffling, I give Mama Rose a hug.

"You are so right, Mama Rose! Whatever would I do without you?" I ask her.

"Well, it would definitely make it easier to keep some of this weight off," Susan laughingly confessed while trying to hide her stomach to make a point. All three of us begin to giggle.

"Now, I think it's time for my cheesecake, don't you think, Wynnie? Made special just for you!" Mama Rose says to me while she takes a chunk of my cheek in her fingers and squeezes.

"I could never pass up your cheesecake! I think I'll even take a piece home to enjoy later on," I answer her with a grin on my face. I just knew she would have some cheesecake for me! What a perfect way to end a very emotionally draining day!

Thank God
He created chocolate!

Chapter 10

WHEN I NEED TIME TO RELAX and reflect on all the chaos happening in my life, there is nothing I like to do more than to watch the sunrise. With my mind whirling at a non-stop pace, sleep is just not happening to me. So with a cup of hot coffee in one hand and my Bible in my other, I head out to my enclosed back porch, curl up in my blanket and watch the sun rise.

Watching a sunrise in the winter is so beautiful! Just as the sun begins to peak over the horizon you can see the mirror of that sun in all the tiny snowflakes covering my backyard. This morning the tiny flakes are swirling in the air due to a slight wind. Watching the shadows begin to lift, the glorious colors start to appear on the backdrop of God's canvas—it is all so beautiful. And so cold! It's a good thing my back porch is enclosed and heated.

There is just so much going through my head lately. From planning this engagement party, to trying to avoid having to deal with some heart issues, and then feeling a little bit of excitement knowing that Rich is still single—I feel like I have lost focus on what is truly important in my life.

I need some God time, and how can I not reflect on Him while watching His masterpiece fill the sky? There is nothing more beautiful than watching the sunrise early in the morning. I have my Bible opened to the book of Psalms. I like to go through the book and find portions of scripture that solely reflect on the majesty and awesomeness of God. When I do this, I find that all those issues that I keep fretting over became nonsense in the eyes of God. Yes, they are important, but saturating myself in the presence of God is more important.

I try to make it a habit to dwell on the praises of God while the sun rises, and then I will allow myself to deal with the issues of my heart. If I can get my priorities straight, then all else will fall into line.

So with that in mind, I finish up my coffee, close my Bible and begin to cry.

After a couple minutes of tears streaming down my face, I begin to search my heart to find out why exactly I was crying. Do I dare to admit that deep in my heart I am feeling hurt by God? Will I be struck with lightening if I say this out loud? Is it possible to feel this way about the one I can call Abba Father?

From what I have read in my devotions today, I am a daughter of God, precious and loved by Him. With this in mind, I think it would be ok to admit my feelings, as long as I am willing to listen to what He has to say to me.

There is so much turmoil in my heart right now. Why is it that we are always told that we need to surrender our uttermost desires to God? Why is it that I am always being reminded that, "My ways are not your ways, thus says the Lord of Hosts"? Why do I need to give up my desires, when all I want is to be loved? I don't want to be single. It's not a choice that I make on a daily decision. I feel like I am paying for a past mistake, one that I made when I was too young to know my own heart. Is it really that terrible to desire a family? How much longer do I have to wait, Father? My internal clock is ticking, and it's been ticking for a while now. If you love me so much, God, then why don't you bring someone into my life that I will love and will love me in return?

I take a deep breath. There, I said it. Now what? I close my eyes and let my head drop towards my lap. I feel resigned. I know in my heart I need to let go of this and move on. I need to find my joy in the Lord. I take another deep breath and prepare to completely surrender—for today at least. Suddenly I get a picture in my mind's eye. It is of my dream when I was on the beach. A picture of being held and hearing sweet words whispered into my ear. I see myself turning around and actually seeing the face of the man who is holding me; the same face that I saw on the website I was looking at the other night. Rich Carradine. The true love of my heart. What does this mean? Am I just confusing what I want with what God wants, or could he possibly be in my future?

I give a little smile and let the image play upon my thoughts for a bit until reality hits.

Reality hits hard. I have just finished pouring the last cup of coffee of the morning. I happened to glance at the clock and realize that it's Sunday, and I have missed the morning service. Thinking back to what I just dealt with this morning, I decided to not feel guilty for playing hooky for once and decided this would be a good time to deal with other issues at hand. The number one issue would be the party. My original thoughts were to hold off until this evening before I began to think of it, but then my thoughts and Nancy's thoughts are apparently on two different wavelengths.

Nancy Montgomery. The very lady my mother believes is gloating over the fact the jilted bride is holding an engagement party for the new bride.

Nancy, who is in a bright pink suit with black pants, walks up my front steps, knocks once on my door and then proceeds to enter into my home.

"Yoo-hoo! Anybody home?" she sings in a sweet, disarming voice.

Thankfully I was presentable. Could you imagine if Nancy entered my home like she did and I was standing there is my unmentionables? If she saw me in my lounge clothes, I would be mortified! No one dares to bask in her presence unless they are in their absolute best. That is just the way Nancy is, a refined social butterfly with horns that are sharper than a freshly sharpened pencil.

"Nancy—what a surprise! I'm in the kitchen," I call out to her as I'm quickly trying to tidy up my messy kitchen, like I can make it appear presentable in the five seconds it will take her to walk down to me!

I can hear the clicking of her shoes as she comes closer. I feel like I'm about to face the firing squad in a few short seconds, and so I take a deep breath, and then a huge sip of my coffee.

Unfortunately, the coffee didn't go down as smoothly as I had hoped, and so I ended up greeting my new guest by having a coughing fit. When I finally looked up from being bent at the waist, I noticed not one but two sets of shoes. One was definitely a high heel and the other, a more comfortable loafer. Nancy did not come alone.

"Hello ladies. Please excuse the mess, I wasn't exactly expecting company this morning," I said to my unexpected guests.

"Wynne! It's so nice to see you. Nancy insisted we had to talk to you, and when we saw you weren't at church this morning, we decided to just pop over here. I hope you don't mind?" greeted the other guest to me, who turned out to be the newly engaged Stacey. Can my day get any better?

"Of course she doesn't mind," interjected Nancy, cutting off my reply that they are always welcome. Perhaps it was a good thing Nancy spoke first. That way I wouldn't be caught in a lie.

I turned to Nancy, stood up straight and decided to face her head on.

"Nancy, what can I do for you?" I asked her. I was polite and forceful, or at least that is how I hope I sounded.

It was a good thing I spent some time with God this morning. Otherwise I would not have the grace and fortitude to deal with this today.

"Well, Wynne, seeing as how you are planning a party for this Friday, I thought it might be best if we came over to help you in any way that you may need. I haven't heard from you yet concerning this, so naturally you must need my help. It is only a few days away, you know. This is too important of a party to leave everything until the last minute, dear," said Nancy to me as she walked around my kitchen. She stopped in front of my large bay window facing out to my backyard. Thankfully there is so much snow on the ground that she is unable to see the disarray that my garden is in. Fixing my gardens is definitely on my to-do list for the spring!

I decided to take the upper hand in all of this. After all, I'm not the one marrying her son, so therefore I don't have to deal with her on a regular basis.

"Oh, Nancy, of course! I should apologize for not getting in touch with you sooner. And Stacey, that goes for you as well. I have had so much on the go that it completely slipped my mind! Of course the mother of the groom and the bride-to-be would have a say in this party!" I exclaimed. Am I pouring it on a little too thick, do you think? Nah!

"Now please don't worry at all. I have a group of ladies who are helping me with this, and everything is all set to go!

Decorations are in order and very tastefully done, food has been delegated to various women, invitations already sent out, and there will even be an announcement in our town paper concerning the party. The church is booked, flowers ordered. Everything down to the tiny detail has been thought of and prepared!" I counted off the lists on my fingers as I announced all I had done so far.

"Well, it certainly sounds like you have everything planned," Nancy said in a quiet voice. I think she was personally hoping to watch me stumble in this. Either that or perhaps she really wanted a hand in organizing this party.

"You can rest assured, Stacey, that this will be a wonderful party!" I addressed Stacey as she looked at me with a perplexed look on her face.

"Nancy, I am even making a special cheesecake and chocolate-dipped strawberries for Friday. I won't disappoint you, I promise." I tried to make it sound more appealing. I'm starting to feel a bit guilty for excluding them from the preparations. Perhaps I was wrong in wanting to do this without Nancy's domineering help.

"Here," I announced. "Why don't you take a seat at the table? I'll put on a fresh pot of coffee, and show you all the notes and pictures of what it will all look like," I asked the two very quiet ladies.

Nancy was able to compose herself quickly. I could see her stiffening up her spine, while Stacey let out an audible breath of relief. I think I managed to save the day!

"That would be lovely," replied Stacey as she took a seat at my small table. Thankfully, there was one space that was neither cluttered nor dirty.

After an hour of explaining and rehashing ideas and decisions, it ended up that both Stacey and Nancy were happy with not only the colors I had chosen, but also with the flowers, food and invitations. Thank goodness I did that right, at least. While I was walking the two ladies to my front door, Stacey gave me a quick hug and thanked me for doing all of this. Nancy, of course just walked out the door without a word, and I managed to close the door with enough dignity to last all of five seconds before I sank to the floor in front of my door in a puddle. It was then that I noticed, that not only did I sink to the floor in a puddle, I also sank right into a puddle of wet snow. Yuck! The perfect ending to a rather harried couple of hours.

After another cup of flavored coffee I decide to do a bit of research on the computer. Of course my first initial reasoning was for party ideas for Friday. But after opening my email, all thoughts of the engagement party dissipated from my mind.

There on the screen was an email message from Rich. I just stared at his name for a second, completely blanking everything else out. He wrote me. He actually wrote me. His email title says "With hopes from Rich." With hopes. Hopes? What type of hopes? With hopes from Rich. What does he mean by that? Ok, I'm hyperventilating now and imagine loud noises ringing in my ears. Take a deep breath. In, out, in, out. The noise is still ringing. I shake my head a bit to clear it, and suddenly realize that the noise I am hearing is my phone. Working on autopilot, I reach out my hand to grab the cordless.

"Hello," I answered, still in somewhat of a daze.

"Wynne? Are you ok?" asked Susan on the other end. I guess she caught the tone of my voice—amazement combined with shock.

"What did you say to him Sue?" I asked her. The shock still hasn't left my voice.

"Say to who Wynne? Whom did I say something to?" Susan asked. Now she's the one with the question in her voice.

"To Rich. What did you say to him Susan? Please tell me!" I begged of her. She had to have said something. Why else would he write me after five long years of silence?

"Wynne, take a deep breathe! I already told you what I said to him, hun. What is wrong? Did something happen? Did you have another dream? Do you need me to come over?" Susan asked me in a bit of a panic.

"No, I don't need you to come over. I had planned on having a nice relaxing day at home getting caught up, remember? So far that hasn't happened, but I'm not going to stop hoping that it does," I said to her a bit testily.

"Ok, then. What is going on, Wynne?" she asked me.

I closed my eyes. Do I really want to tell her? Maybe this is just a dream and the email really isn't there. I open my eyes. Nope, it's not a dream.

"I just received an email from Rich. After five years of silence, and one year of you hounding me to contact him, I get an email from him! Why would he be writing me, Susan? Why now, of all times?" I asked her with a hint of a beg in that question.

"Oh, Wynne. What does it say? Have you read it? Read it to me!" she demanded, as if I dare keep a secret from her.

"I haven't read it yet, Sue. It's just sitting there in my inbox as an unopened new message. I'm not sure if I really want to open it. What if he just writes to say hi and that's it. What do I say back?"

"What does the message title say, Wynne?" Susan asked me in a quiet voice.

"With hopes from Rich," I answered her.

There was silence at the other end of the phone for a couple of seconds. Those seemed like the longest seconds in my life!

"With hope? With hope," you could hear Susan mutter on the other line.

"I think you should go ahead and open it, Wynne. If he mentions hope, that has to be a good thing!" Susan encouraged me.

"Well, of course I'm going to open it! But I think I need to be fortified with some chocolate first," I told her. There's no way that I can make it through this life-changing email without some chocolate.

"You and chocolate! Just hurry up and call me back! You can't leave me in suspense for too long, else you know what will happen," she warned me. Boy is she right! Susan doesn't handle suspense very well. The last time I left her hanging for something less momentous than this, she left work early to come over and demand to know what had happened. Needless to say, although I hung up on her due to a fact of brownies left too long in the oven, I learned my lesson about not keeping things from her.

After finding some hidden chocolate bars in my cupboard (yes, I hide them from myself!) I get up enough nerve to sit back down at the computer and open up the message from Rich.

Message: *With hopes from Rich.*

Surprise, Wynne. Sitting here writing to you, I find it hard to believe that it has actually been almost five years since I last saw you. I pray that this finds you well. I spoke with Susan recently, and she mentioned how you have made your dreams become a reality. Good for you, Wynne. I'm so proud of you! Susan also made mention that you are not married.

Hearing that brought to mind some memories and dreams that we both had once upon a time. I know I'm being a bit presumptuous, but I am hoping that you will take the plunge with me. I miss you, Wynne. I would like to build upon the friendship that we once used to have. I'm hoping you would like to do the same.

Sincerely,
Rich

I have to be dreaming! This chocolate that is melting in my mouth must be part of my dream. There's no way that my heart can be beating this fast, butterflies be swirling in my belly at this rate and this not be a dream! He actually wrote me!

I quickly begin to write him a reply before I face reality and become too much of a chicken. I give myself a quick pep talk—don't appear too anxious or eager; play it cool.

Dear Rich:
  What a surprise! It is so nice to hear from you. I agree, it's hard to believe that so much time has gone by. I would enjoy rebuilding our friendship— you have also been on my heart and mind lately. You were always better at taking these plunges than I was.

*Do you remember when we used to email each
other, only to find out that we were both online at the
same time? We'd then head over to our favorite
coffee shop and spend time together. Those were the
days!*

*Behave yourself, and I look forward to hearing
from you soon. We have so much to get caught up on.*

The girl with the dreams—Wynne

There, not too gushy, but enough memories of our past to
show him that I remember and am interested. I used to always
personalize my ending to him. Rich once told me that he looked
forward to seeing how I would end my letters or emails to him;
he said he could catch a glimpse into my heart that way.

Now, do I have the nerve and the gumption to send this?
Only one tiny hit of the send button and this will be out of my
hands. Am I ready for this? This will mean that the possibility
of my dreams coming true is one more step out of my comfort
zone.

I press the send button and watch the screen tell me that
my message has been sent. I feel exhausted. Just one little
action took so much emotional energy—I definitely need
another piece of chocolate now.

Tomorrow I will start to diet.

When you dream of
chocolate, it always
comes true.

Chapter 11

I HAD THOUGHTS OF STARTING THE DAY off bright and early. I had my alarm set at a decent enough time to make some coffee and have a long shower, perhaps try one of the muffins I took out of the freezer, spend some time with the kittens and then head to the store in a nice frame of mind.

My thoughts, however, are generally just dreams, I have come to find.

Just as I am pouring my coffee and heating up a muffin, the phone rings. Even before I manage to squeak out a, "Good morning," I hear a demanding voice coming from the other line.

"What happened to you last night? Why didn't you phone me? Matt told me I had to wait until this morning to find out what happened with your email," Susan greets me in her typical fashion—fast and furious.

"Good morning to you too, Sue! Gee, it's so nice to talk to you this early in the morning. You definitely know how to make one's day bright and sunny," I tease her. I don't really know if I'm ready to share the email with her just yet.

All last night I felt like I was living in a dream world. The concept that he wants to renew our friendship, if nothing else, amazed me. I went to sleep with a smile on my face. My dreams were filled with romance, you know, the kind where you actually get to see the face of the man you are in love with.

"Augh, Wynne! Come on, tell me about the email!" Susan demanded in a rather disgusted tone of voice. I guess she's not in the mood to play games this morning.

I decided to tease her a bit. I know just how much she hates that!

"Oh, you know, a little bit of this and a little bit of that. Nothing too serious, just hi, how are you, kind of thing," I tell her with a 'who cares' type of voice.

"What do you mean 'that kind of thing'? Come on, Wynne. Play nice here! After all, I did let you sleep last night instead of calling you at all hours just to find out. Wynne, come on now, you have just got to tell me!" Susan questioned, demanded and then pleaded with me.

Oh, how I love to tease her! It has become a pastime that I quite enjoy now and again.

"Oh, alright. Tell you what. Meet me at the store and I'll tell you all about it over fresh coffee and muffins," I told her, just to keep the suspense a little longer.

"Oh, you! Fine! I'll see you soon." I could hear the exasperation in her voice as she hung up. I do love to tease her!

The forecast said to expect a lot of snow today so I took the time to shovel my walkway and made sure the heat was on for the kittens before I left for the store. Now if they can only behave while I'm gone... then that will be a miracle! Thankfully it wasn't too icy out this morning as I walked to my car, arms laden with Tupperware containers full of muffins and my idea book. The engagement party for Jude and Stacey is on Friday, only a few days away. Hard to believe how quickly this has caught up with me. This week I will need to finalize what everyone is bringing, the little things I might have forgotten, and make sure I incorporate all the ideas Nancy and Stacey want added. The Latte Ladies will be meeting the day before the party. What would I do without those ladies? Thankfully I'll never have to find out.

As I pull up to the store, I notice Susan has already made it ahead of me. I give a little chuckle as I try to grab the muffins with one hand while twisting sideways to get out of my car. Without much thought I swing both feet out of the car into the huge pile of snow right at the car door. I can literally feel the snow squishing up into my pants. Just great. Why didn't I wear my boots today? Now my feet are all soaked, and my hands are too full to do anything about the snow up my pants.

Susan is at the door of the shop waiting for me to come in. The little chicken won't come out here to help me, but she'll take the muffins from me when I get to her. Nice friend I have! I try to shake my feet with each step that I take, hoping to dislodge some of the snow stuck up my pants. With each jiggle,

I can feel the muffin containers slide, yet I'm so into the process of doing my little dance that I am unable to stop the total muffin avalanche that is about to occur. Just as I place my one foot down on what I thought would be an ice-free sidewalk, I quickly realize that it isn't, in fact, completely ice free.

Not only do the muffins slide to the ground only to be lost in the snow, but my foot also decides to follow suit along the ice-covered sidewalk and I join my muffins in the snow. When I say that I joined the muffins in the snow, I mean that quite literally—I landed right on top of the muffins. I look up, hoping to find Susan there with a helping hand, and all I see is Susan bent over at the waist laughing at me. Not helping me, but laughing hysterically. One hand is covering her mouth while the other one is half stretched out towards me pointing towards the ground. I think she is laughing so hard that she can't keep her arm out straight for me to grasp.

"Susan! Would you stop laughing and get over here! This isn't funny!" I called to her. I try to get up, but my foot keeps slipping, and the muffins are in the way of me getting a firm grasp on the ground to support me up.

I look over at my would-be rescuer, and instead of finding her coming towards me, she is still stuck in the doorway laughing.

"SUSAN! THIS IS NOT FUNNY!" I yell while trying not to laugh. Actually, it is quite funny. I'm half covered in snow, soaking wet now, and sitting on a pile of muffins all the while, unable to get up. Good thing these muffins are in Tupperware containers, or else they would be mush by now.

"Oh, come on now, let me help you," Susan says to me as she reaches her hand out and helps to pull me up. She finally left the sanctuary of the store to help me in my time of crisis!

"What a true friend you are, Sue. Thanks so much," I say to her sarcastically. If she had come out sooner, I wouldn't be this wet.

"Well, at least I put on the coffee," she said to me. When I glance at her, she proceeds to stick out her tongue. What childish behavior! I just shake my head and plop the containers of muffins in her arms and then march off to the bathroom to clean up.

As I heavily thump across the floor to the washroom, I can hear Susan whistling, "It's beginning to look a lot like Christmas," in the background. I turn and give her a good glare. She gives me an innocent look and then giggles at me. I look down at myself and see puddles of snow forming at my feet where I stand.

"Just for that," I say to her, "you can clean up the floor!"

It took me longer than I thought to clean myself up and look presentable. After drying myself off as best I could with the dryer in the bathroom and then cleaning up my mess with paper towels on the floor, I walk out of the bathroom and can hear the doorbells jingling.

"Good morning, Sunshine!" I hear a booming voice greet me from the door. I instantly feel myself perk up and rush over to the man that just arrived.

"Dad! I've missed you! How are you feeling?" I asked him as I gave him a big hug. My father is one of those blessings in my life that I continually thank God for. Last year he suffered a heart attack that no one thought he would survive from. I thought for sure that I had lost my father, and it was all I could do not to break apart. But he is more stubborn than we all thought he was and pulled through with no complications. He has since semi-retired from being retired and has developed a habit of coming into the store a few mornings a week to start his day. He claims it is to try out my coffees before I poison the unsuspecting souls that come into my store each day. I personally think it is to get away from my mom for a few moments of solitude.

"Not too bad for being an old man, not too bad," he says as he hugs me back.

"Good to hear! Susan put on the coffee this morning, so I can guarantee you that it's probably ruined already, but it's fresh," I say to him as I walk with him to the coffee bar.

"Hey!" says Susan. "I heard that! You're just jealous because you know Jack loves my coffee more than yours. Don't you?" she says to my dad as she gives him a little punch in the arm.

"Now, now, girls," my dad admonishes.

"You both know how I feel about your coffee. Why do you think I come in so often? Someone has to test it before you allow others to try it!" he teased us as he poured himself a cup of French Roast.

"You should really try one of our flavored coffees, Dad," I suggest to him.

"Now why go and ruin a good thing?" he answered back as he stirred sugar into his cup.

I poured myself a coffee and followed my dad to the corner table with the comfy chairs. This is exactly what I love about my store, the coziness and comfort of being able to feel wrapped up in warmth while sipping my favorite flavored beverage.

"So how are you, Dad?" I asked him after a few moments of silence.

"Well, Sunshine, I'm doing alright. It's you I'm a little concerned about," he told me as he placed his mug down on the table.

"Oh Dad, not you too!" I sighed.

"Yes, Sugar, me as well. I know you have had a time the past little bit, but there is something I want to talk to you about. This thing here that you gave your crazy mother permission to do was the most foolish thing you could have done!" He admonished me while picking up his coffee.

"What thing, Dad? I'm lost! If you mean making some desserts for the party tomorrow, what was wrong with that?" I asked him, a bit puzzled.

"No, not the desserts! You know your mother makes the best squares around! The only thing I ever complain about with that is she doesn't make enough for me to have!" He pouted while taking a bite of his muffin.

"She's still keeping you on a tight leash, is she, Dad?" I asked him with a chuckle.

"Well she won't listen to me that a little bit of sweets every once in a while can't hurt somebody," he complained.

"No, that wasn't what I was talking about, Wynne girl. This mystery date that she has lined up for you! That foolish thing," he told me.

"What mystery date, Dad? Why would I let Mom set up a mystery date for me?" I was even more puzzled now.

"What do you mean? You don't remember? The guy she has escorting you to the party Friday night, Wynne! That date! Don't tell me you don't remember giving your stubborn mother the heads up to do that!" he cried out in exasperation.

"Oh, the date! Honestly, Dad, I had completely forgotten about that! What's wrong with it? It's harmless. I made mom promise not to get any notions in her head, seeing as this will only be for one night. Dad, I'm going to be so busy, that I will hardly have any time for the guy on that night. I actually feel sorry for him!" I explained to him. I really didn't see it as that big of a deal.

"You have no idea, do you?" he asked me with a note of surprise in his voice.

"No idea about what? Dad, what is going on?" I asked him. Now I'm starting to get a bit nervous.

"I promised your mother that I wouldn't ruin her surprise, and you know your mom! It'll be the end of me if I do. But I just want to make sure that you are prepared for what she has done. This isn't a guy that you can brush off, Wynne!" Dad warned me.

"Ok," I say hesitantly.

"I'm serious, Wynne. Do your old dad a favor will you?" he asked me.

"Should I be worried, Dad? I just said yes to Mom to make her feel better," I said to him.

"Well, when it comes to your Mother, you should know by now nothing is simple. I want you to promise me something. Can you do that?" Dad again asked me.

"Ok, what do you want me to do?" I asked him. I'm really starting to freak out now.

"Promise your old Dad that you won't shrug this guy off! Dress up really nice, Wynne, prepare yourself for an awesome date. Don't brush him off so you can do this party. Please? Will you do that for me?" It was almost as if he was begging me.

"Ok, Dad. I promise! I'll wear my best outfit and dazzle him with my smile. I'll make Mom so happy that she will be floating. But I want you to promise me something, Dad," I said to him. This was going to be a give and take situation. If I have to give a lot to some guy that my mom feels is 'right' for me, then Dad is going to have to give as well.

"I knew you would try to bargain with this! Alright, what do I have to promise?" he replied in a tone of resignation.

"I want you to promise me that you will come to the party with Mom! Now, don't you be shaking your head at me! Jude is not the bad guy here, Dad, and it's time you let up on being protective of me with this. I mean it Dad! It's been three long years, and you need to forgive him for hurting your little girl. Please?" I begged him.

My dad is a wonderful man, very loving, generous and funny. But watch out if you hurt someone he loves! He becomes very protective and has a hard time forgetting. He has blamed everything on Jude for the past three years. I, of course, have never told him the truth, but I have tried to get him to let it all go.

"Wynne, don't get into this. You already know how I feel about Jude. The least he could have done was be man enough and stick around to help clear the mess instead of running like a ninny and make you deal with it all," Dad said to me in his gruff voice. This as always has been a sore spot between us.

"It wasn't his fault," I find myself whispering.

"Of course it was his fault, Wynne! Stop taking the blame for him," my dad replied with his voice rising ever so slightly.

I dropped my head and stared at the floor.

"No, Dad. It wasn't his fault. It was because of me the wedding was called off. I broke his heart." Oh my, I can't believe I'm actually admitting this to my father. I haven't said anything in three years. I have just let him believe that I was the one needing protection.

I lifted my head slightly to look at my father. He was just sitting there in stunned silence. Neither one of us said anything for a few moments, yet it felt like eternity.

"Are you telling me that you were the one to call off the wedding?" He asked with a hint of incredibility to his voice.

"It was a mutual decision, Dad. Jude asked me to give him something that I couldn't give. He wanted my whole heart, Dad, and I couldn't give that to him! So, instead of settling, we both sort of made the decision to not get married. You can't fault him for taking off like he did," I admitted to him in a catchy voice. Part of me felt relief at being able to finally admit this to my dad, but the rest of me felt shame for letting him down.

"So you were still in love with that Richard guy from school, is that what you are really saying? I thought you got over him, Wynne. Why wouldn't you tell me this before now? I'm your father, Wynne. I'll love you no matter what, you know that!" There was a wrenching sound to my father's voice as he told me he loved me.

I took a deep sigh and raised my head.

"I just didn't want to disappoint you, Dad," I whispered to him.

My father appeared to be choked up for a few moments.

"Ah, Wynne, honey—you will never be a disappointment to me!" He said as he took my hand in his and lightly rubbed it.

So this is how receiving a father's love feels. Like you are surrounded by warmth, acceptance and love. Knowing that no matter what, that love will never change. Almost like a little girl who climbs up into her daddy's lap, knowing that she will always receive love from her daddy.

I have always been a bit fearful of what it would feel like once my dad found out the truth about the cancelled wedding. I thought he would be so disappointed in me that he would lose his trust in me. Just the thought always hurt me to the core. Perhaps that is why I have been so willing to live in the past, in my dreams and not facing reality. Once I stood up and decided to face what happened and move on, then I would have to accept the truth of my actions. Perhaps I've never been able to really forgive myself, thus placing part of that blame on God because it was just easier. It is easier to live in the 'what if' instead of living in today and embracing it.

While I was silently contemplating this new thought I could hear my father talk under his breathe.

"So your mother isn't that much of a nutcase after all then!"

"Pardon me, Dad?" I asked him.

"Hmm, oh nothing honey, just talking to myself!" he replied.

With that my dad stood up, drank the last bit of his coffee and prepared to leave.

"Now, you just remember what you promised me, Wynne! I think you'll find that you may just like your mystery man after all," he chuckled as he drew me into a hug.

I felt a bit puzzled and I'm sure I had the facial expression to show it, but dad just gave me a quick wave and left the store whistling a tune.

I could hear Susan come up behind me.

"What was that about?" she asked me.

"I have no idea!" I confessed to her, still feeling a bit puzzled.

"One minute everything was serious, and then the next he's chuckling and saying weird things about my mom. Don't ask me!" I said to her in reply to her questioning look.

"Honestly, Wynne, sometimes I tend to wonder about your family," was Susan's answer to me as she shook her head.

I just stuck my tongue out at her.

"It takes one to know one!" was my sassy reply.

"And wouldn't you know!" Susan shot back at me while grabbing my hand. She quickly tugged me back into the chair that I had just vacated and pushed me down.

"Now, before another person enters this store, I want to hear about that email!" Susan demanded as she stood above me with her hands on her hips.

"Someone's getting a wee bit pushy, aren't they?" I asked her with a smile on my lips.

"Wynne!" Susan growled at me.

"Alright, alright, sit down and I'll let you in on what he said," I said soothingly in hopes of placating her.

As I proceeded to tell Susan all that Richard had written to me, we had two customers come into the store. Susan quickly looked up and told the ladies that we would be with them soon, and then made me finish my story. Amidst her little squeals when I told her what he wrote and her little giggles when I confessed my extra need for chocolate when I sent my reply, I managed to get the whole story out in time to speak to the customers that continued to arrive despite the amount of snow that was steadily adding up on the piles already formed on the ground.

Time to put on more coffee and get the Christmas music started!

Chocolate
is the best gift
to give.

Chapter 12

WHY IS IT YOU NEVER REALIZE you are having a crazy day until the day is basically over? With all the morning mishaps and busyness, I should have clued in that the day would not get any better, no matter how much chocolate one consumed!

Thankfully the store stayed quite busy during the morning, so I didn't have time to ponder my father's bizarre behavior and request. Nor was I able to focus on the party at all. With less than a month to Christmas I can't seem to keep my shelves stocked. My goal is to give people ideas apart from the normal bath towels, kitchen gadgets and plates. Instead, they come into Chocolate Blessings and find an assortment of wall décor, interesting table pieces, one of a kind ornaments and handmade items. I love to gaze at the customers as they casually peruse the shelves until they find the one item that just catches their eye. They will stop and gasp, tentatively reach out to stroke the item, look it over and cradle it in the palm of their hand. When I see the contented look on their face, then I am happy. Today, I saw that look so many times that I felt I was floating on air. We ran out of the roses that we give to each customer before lunch. When Lily came in for her afternoon shift I quickly ran to the florist beside us and bought more roses as well as a couple arrangements to place throughout the store. This time I managed not to slip and fall.

Right after lunch Jude and Stacey came into the store. You could just see that these two were a couple in love. With all the loving glances, little touches and the fact that they stuck to each other's side like glue, one would have to have been blind not to notice. The ring on Stacey's left hand also showed this to be a fact. The way it would sparkle and shine when she moved her hand, and the 'oh and ah' you could hear from all those who noticed was just another signal that love was in the air.

"Stacey!" I called out to her while the pair slowly walked over to the counter.

"You just hurry over here and let me see that ring!" I demanded when she kept taking her time. What woman doesn't want to ogle an engagement ring, especially when that woman happens to be single?

"Wynne! Isn't it gorgeous?" Stacey gushed to me while extending her arm so her ring was right in front of my face. Honestly, she could have kept the ring at her side and I still would have seen the beauty of it.

"That is gorgeous!" I exclaimed as I took her hand and carefully looked at her ring. WOW. Gorgeous doesn't even describe it.

"Yep, Jude outdid himself, that's for sure!" she said as she took her hand back and twirled it around in the air.

When Jude proposed to me, he gave me his grandmother's heirloom ring with the promise that he would buy me a ring deserving of his love later on. I was happy with the heirloom. I of course returned it after we called our wedding off, and at times I still remember how it looked, so regal and full of history. But this ring is definitely a ba-da-bing type of ring. A pear diamond, surrounded by tiny diamonds, on a sparking gold band. Very beautiful, and, I have to admit, the sight of it is making me a little jealous.

"Really, Jude, that is a beautiful ring!" I said to him as others in the store began to surround the pair to gaze at its beauty.

I stood there watching as Stacey showed off her ring, and noticed after a few moments that Jude was coming towards me.

"Um, Wynne," he begins a bit hesitantly.

"Hey, that is beautiful, and she deserves it," I said to him, hoping to get rid of the awkward feeling between us.

"Thanks. Listen, about Friday night, I just want to say thank you. I know that this isn't the ideal situation, but you've really outdone yourself on planning this for us," Jude said to me as he twiddled with his thumbs.

"Um, Wynne," he began again.

"Yes," I answered. Obviously he has something to say, so I'll be nice and not interrupt him.

"Wynne, your dad came by this morning to see me. He told me that he needed to apologize to me. I thought we had agreed not to tell anyone about what happened, especially our parents, Wynne? I'm not upset, but the least you could have done was warn me! My mom heard us talking, and now she wants to have a talk with me!" Jude told me in an agitated voice. Good to see I'm not the only one who cowers before his mom.

"Oh, Jude, I'm sorry!" I said to him.

"I didn't even think about warning you. I had no idea that he would even say anything to you. It just came out this morning. I didn't want him to blame you anymore for something that wasn't even your fault," I confessed to him.

"It's alright, it was just a bit awkward. I mean, your dad, Wynne, apologized to me, when really it should have been me apologizing to him!" Jude stated.

"Jude, we've already been through this. It's out of the bag now. I had to tell my dad, so you're going to have to deal with your mom, although I wouldn't wish that on my neighbor's dead cat! It's in the past, history, lets not rehash this again, ok?" I said to him with a hint of weariness to my voice. I really am tired of dealing with all this. I feel like I've been rung inside out with dealing with all the emotional baggage towards my dad, God and myself. Enough is enough.

"Plus, about tomorrow—really it's no big deal. There are enough people involved with this now that it really isn't me putting on this party for you and Stacey, it has basically become a church event. So the people you need to thank are those that loved you and taught you about Jesus your whole life," I told him.

"Are you sure?" Jude asked me.

"Absolutely positive! Now go and stand beside your fiancé before she notices that you are gone," I told him as I pushed him away with my hands.

"So you're really doing ok?" I hear a voice behind me say.

I literally jumped and gave a quiet little shriek.

"Augh! Susan! Do you have to sneak up behind people like that?" I say to her while gently swatting at her arm.

"In order to get the truth in a timely fashion with you, yes, as a matter of fact, I do!" Susan replied saucily to me as she swatted me back.

"Don't you know it's rude to eavesdrop?" I replied to her.

"When has that ever stopped me?" Susan asked me.

"Hmm, now that is true!" I answered her. We then both began to laugh.

Lily came to take care of the counter, so Susan and I both grabbed a fresh cup of coffee and went to sit in the back office to chat. Much to my surprise, the office was already occupied.

"Well hey there, stranger!" I said to Matt.

Matt had somehow managed to slip past me this morning without my even noticing. He looked happy as he sat back in the desk chair completely surrounded by mounds of paper and a half full cup of coffee.

"Hey there, Wynne. Guess Sue forgot to mention I was back here, eh?" he said to me as he looked adoringly at his wife.

"Are you having fun?" I asked him as I took a look at the papers on the desk.

"You betcha! We're actually doing really well this month," Matt informed me.

I had completely forgotten, but today was Matt's day to come in and work on the books, something that I just dread having to do. It does feel good, though, to hear Matt tell me how good we are doing, something I know in my heart, but now it's actually on paper.

"I've noticed that we're getting a little bit low on stock, Wynne. I transferred a bunch of money into the PayPal account. Do you think you could do some quick ordering from your crafty ladies?" Matt asked me as he motioned with his arm toward the depleting stock that we have sitting on the shelves behind him.

"With planning the party, I guess I got behind a bit. Sorry. I don't think it will be a problem. I'm expecting a box to come any day with some great Christmas items and more candles. I'll definitely order some more tonight, though," I said to him as I began to peek in the boxes to see what we had left to stock shelves with.

I looked up to find Susan sitting on her husband's lap. She was whispering something in his ear. Just as I was about to make a comment to them on their coziness, Matt interrupted me.

"I think I'll run and grab us some lunch. You ladies have a good chat and please make sure you're done by the time I get back! I'll bring back some Chinese food if you behave yourselves," Matt promised as he began to zip up his jacket and walk towards the door.

"What did you say to him?" I asked her as we both sat down.

"Oh, just that we needed to have a girly chat and that I was craving some Chinese food," she said to me with a wink. Since being married, I've noticed that Matt and Susan seem to have their own personal language that I don't understand at all.

"So what were the magic words, *girly chat* or *Chinese food?*" I asked her.

Susan just laughed at me.

"So, are you really doing ok?" she asked me, completely ignoring my earlier question.

That was the hint that it's time for some serious talk now. I took a sip of coffee and laid my heart bare before her.

"Yes, Susan. I really and truly am doing ok now. I've been having some real heart to heart discussions with God, dealing with a lot of garbage that was buried inside. I think admitting to my dad what happened with Jude really helped this morning. When my dad told me that he would never be disappointed in me, it was like a huge weight lifted off of my shoulders. I believe it also opened up a section of my heart that I've been hiding from God as well," I told her.

"Wow. That's great, Wynne! You know whenever our Pastor talks about the Father's Love on Sundays, he often mentions that our views of God as our Father, or Abba, come from our relationships with our earthly fathers," Susan reminded me in an encouraging way.

"I know. I thought of that as well. It's so true Susan. I used to think that there was a difference; that we could separate the two if we really wanted, but I don't think that is possible in our hearts. How we respond and react with our own dads really does control how we respond to God as our heavenly father. I realized that this morning," I admitted to her.

"Don't forget the fact that you received an email from a good looking dream guy! That always helps to heal the heart," Susan said to me with a huge smile on her face.

"Hmm, we mustn't forget that!" I said to her tongue in cheek. She knows me so well.

"Speaking of a handsome dream guy, did you dream about him last night by any chance?" Susan asked me with a sly look in her eye.

"Actually, no. Isn't that funny? I thought for sure I would, especially after receiving his email. But it was just a deep, peaceful sleep for me last night," I told her thoughtfully. I'd never even noticed my dreamless sleep this morning.

"Hmmm, I wonder what that means?" Susan asked me.

"Oh, you!" I said to her, knowing she was just trying to tease me. I could tell Susan had more on her mind, but thankfully Matt knocked on the door and poked his head in at the perfect time.

"Is it safe to enter now? I brought goodies," Matt said as he waved a bag of Chinese food in the air.

"Hmmm, lunch time! You can enter in anytime as long as you come bearing food!" I called out to him.

I glance over at Susan in time to see her give a little pout and then glance quickly back at Matt and see him give a little shrug. Hmm, I wonder what is going on between these two?

After a delicious lunch of chicken fried rice, chicken balls, beef stir fry and an egg roll, I decided to take the afternoon and work on replacing our depleting stock. Knowing that Lily would stay until closing, I felt fairly confident that I would be leaving the store in good hands. With teasing remarks to watch out for the snow, Susan and Matt both push me out. Susan's excuse was to check my email right away and to call her as soon as I heard back from Richard. Matt only wanted me out of the office so that I could order more stock.

Watching carefully where I stepped on my way to the car, I found myself wishing that Richard had written me back already. I felt like a silly little schoolgirl waiting to receive her first love note from a boy; giddy and foolish. I loved this feeling; it was new yet felt comfortable, like an old pair of sneakers. I had no idea where this feeling was going to lead me, but I really hoped I could be like Dorothy following the yellow brick road.

When I arrived home I immediately got into comfort mode. Fresh pot of coffee brewing, comfy pants and sweater with my hair pulled back. After searching everywhere for my slippers I looked for the trail that the kittens like to create with their findings. I've noticed with Cocoa and Jewel that they have created their very own treasure chest amongst the many boxes in my bedroom closet. If there is an item I cannot find, it is almost guaranteed that it will be in this chest they created. There is an old shoebox that I keep full of little things that bring back memories for me. I have a shell that I found at the beach once. I love the sound of soothing waves, seagulls flying overhead. It's a very peaceful feeling for me, and so I keep this shell to remind me of that sense of peace. There are also beads from a broken necklace that my first best friend from grade school bought me. Little things like that. Well the kittens have also decided to claim this box as their own. I find socks, shoelaces, washcloths, and cotton balls in there. It appears that today their newest find is my slipper. I walk into my room calling out the kittens' names. I can hear a slight meowing. Opening my closet door I find one kitten curled up in a ball inside my slipper and the other is lying on top of the foot part. Adorable. Not adorable enough for me to forgo wearing my slippers, though.

When I log on to my online forums, I find the hours tend to fly by before I eventually come up for breath. I can drink a whole pot of coffee and not realize it. First ,I go through the various threads, catching up on people's lives. Then I get down to business. I have a list of my favorite vendors, but I always try to find new business that are created, wanting to give them a chance to expand and realize their dreams. I browse the new sites first, making lists of prices and items that I like. I love it when I can find a whole assortment of items at one site, but there have been times when I see only a few creations that I know will be a success in my store. This normally takes an hour or so to do. Then I bring out the big guns—my "favorites" list. This is the part I love. I find out their new items and pick my favorites, then go through and reorder the tried and true items that keep selling. I can literally spend hours doing this. I also browse some online auctions. The majority of the ladies on the forums all have eBay auctions that run continually, and if I can catch them at the right time, I can grab those goodies. There's nothing like waiting until the very last minute of an auction and placing your bid in at the exact second before it closes! The thrill of the hunt gets me every time.

Before I log on to do some work, I find myself eagerly opening up my inbox to see if I have any new messages awaiting me. Sure enough, the message that I was hoping for has arrived! I can feel the flutters begin to happen in my stomach, my heartbeat starts racing and I begin to feel very nervous. What will he say? How will he respond to my message? What will happen next? I find myself taking a deep breath.

> *My dreaming Wynne;*
>
> *You always had the best dreams. Good to know that hasn't changed. I remember the days we would meet for coffee. I hear you have a quaint coffee area in your store. Perhaps I'll surprise you one day and drive down to see you. Then we can get all caught up and you can show me how all your dreams came true.*
>
> *It's hard to misbehave when you are a teacher, Wynne. Growing up is hard work, but an opportunity has come into my life that will allow me to explore all those things I let go of so long ago. It would be nice if you could experience this with me.*
>
> *So tell me about a dream you've had recently?*
>
> *Always curious—Rich*

I slowly let go of the breath I am holding in and feel a huge smile spread across my face. I close my eyes. I can barely allow myself to believe this. Richard was always so good at leaving little messages within a vague message. I'm not sure if I dare to actually read into what he wrote. Is he actually suggesting the possibility of a future between us? Would he really come down to see me? Doesn't he remember how much I detest surprises?

I immediately give Susan a call at the store. I'm so excited that there is no way I can keep this to myself. I need someone to squeal with me!

"Wynne!!!! He's coming to see you! That is so exciting!" was Susan's response when I read her the email over the phone.

"Sue, I'm so excited! I can't quite believe this. I have no idea when he'll be coming," I whined to her.

"Well, we'll just have to make sure you look stunning every day, that way you'll be prepared no matter when he comes," she told me in a very practical manner.

"And are you prepared to come over and make me look stunning every day?" I asked her back just a bit sarcastically.

"Darling, you can't expect me to perform miracles everyday!" Susan told me in her best diva voice. We both had a quick laugh.

"Seriously, Wynne. This could be your dream come true. Are you ready?" she asked me, all joking aside.

"Right now, Sue, I'm too excited to think about what all this means! I think I'll just bask in the thought of it all coming true for now. I'll deal with him coming to see me when it actually happens. Who knows, it could be after the New Year for all I know," I told her.

"Oh come on, Wynne. For a guy who was so in love with you that he still wants to find out if the spark could still be there, *as if* he would wait until after Christmas! You should know him better than that. Richard is the type that once he decides what he wants, he goes after it full force. Or have you forgotten that about him?" Susan asked me.

"People can change, you know." I told her. What if he has changed? What if he decides that he wants to take his time and not give me the chance to win back his heart? What if he decides I'm not worth it? Why am I letting the unknown bother me so much?

"Snap out of it, Wynne! You know…" Susan was saying to me before I could hear Matt garbling something in the background to her.

"Wynne, I ah, I need to go. Matt needs me. Bye," Susan said to me as she quickly hung up the phone. Hmm, wonder what that was all about?

I quickly dismiss from my mind my conversation with Susan and decide to get down to work. The first order of business for tonight is to place some more orders for stock, and then I'll indulge and think about the email I just received. It's not very often that Matt gives me the go-ahead to do a free-for-all in orders, so I had better get it done tonight before he changes his mind! After the work is done, then I'll allow myself to dream.

Nothing tastes better than
Mom's Ole Fashioned
Chocolate Cake.

Chapter 13

AFTER SPENDING AN EXHAUSTING DAY at Chocolate Blessings, I decided to change my schedule a bit and have a relaxing bath before I made dinner. With the engagement party coming up fast, I have a feeling that tonight will be just as busy as the day was with last minute phone calls and such. While making dinner, I began to reflect on the day's occurrences. The morning started off fairly slow, with only a few regulars coming into the shop for their morning coffee. I had quite a few orders come in today that I had placed last month, so with things being so quiet, I decided to go through the new stock and take inventory. After the first box, I realized that the shipment that was received was completely different from the one I had ordered. After trying to find invoices and websites, then trying to unsuccessfully get ahold of the vendor who sold me the items, I was beginning to feel a little frazzled. To end the day, a mother came in with her two rambunctious boys who literally caused a whirlwind tornado atmosphere to fill the store and I had to spend a few hours trying to clean up their mess.

Needless to say, I was looking forward to getting home and relaxing in my own little world.

With that thought, I was just about to turn the ringer off my phone when it began to ring. I answer with a tentative hello.

"Wynne! Why don't you come over for dinner tonight?" my mother asked me on the other line. I love going over to my parents' place for dinner. Any night that I don't have to cook for myself is a treat, but when it comes to my mom's homemade food, it becomes a special treat.

"Mom, I'd love to, but tonight's not the best night. I was just about to take a bath and then work on the last minute preparations for the party on Friday," I explained to her.

"I thought you might be working on that tonight, that's why I have dinner in the oven. I thought I could help you. Two minds are always better than one. Besides, you know how much

I love parties!" Mom said to me as she tried to twist my arm into coming.

"Go, have your bath, and by the time you get here, the lasagna will be ready," she continued.

"Hmmm, lasagna! How can I say no to that? Do you want me to grab something for dessert?" I asked her. I love my mother's lasagna!

"No need, I already made a chocolate cake! Go have your bath and then come on over. Make sure you turn off your phone during your bath!" she told me. My mom knows me so well.

"Actually, Mom, I was just about to do that when you called," I told her with a laugh.

"Well then, what are you doing still on the phone? Bye," she said to me as she hung up.

I just shook my head. I often wonder about my mom. She's definitely a unique individual. Good thing she has my father around to keep her feet firmly on the ground.

I manage to scoot out the kittens from playing with the toilet paper in the bathroom and begin filling up the tub. I always keep a large selection of bath items in a basket on the cupboard. Vanilla, coconut and strawberry are the essential scents that I have right now, and every so often I like to add a mixture of different scents. The scent that I use all depends on the mood I am in. With the phone turned off, and bubbles in the tub, I light the candles I have in the bathroom and go to find the latest book that I am reading. No chocolate for me tonight—I need to keep room for the lasagna and cake. So much for that diet I wanted to start. Guess I will have to start after the party is done.

I arrive at my parent's home just in time to see a florist van pull up in front of the house. As I walk up the pathway I see my mom is waiting at the door for me holding a large arrangement of flowers in her hand. I see her casually look at the card and then place it in her pant pocket. She smiles at me as I walk in.

"Those are beautiful flowers, Mom! Who are they from?" I asked her as I bent slightly to smell the bouquet.

My father walks up behind me, places his arm casually around my shoulders and asks the same question.

"Who sent you flowers, dear?" he asked her as he tried to see if there was a card to read.

"Oh, you know, just a secret admirer." Mom announced as she smiled and gave my dad one of those secret looks that are shared between couples.

My father wrinkled his forehead as he tried to think.

"Secret admirer? Who would be sending you... oh... a secret admirer!" he said with a hint of secrecy in his voice.

All right, now I'm intrigued.

"Why do you have a secret admirer, Mom? I asked her.

"Why does anyone have a secret admirer, dear?" she asked me in a faraway tone as she walked into the kitchen. I just gave my father a look; he shrugged his shoulders and then proceeded to walk into the living room where I could hear the low tone of the television. I listen for a few seconds and then hear the common gunshots of a western show being played. I smile, knowing that some things never change. You'll always find my mother either in her kitchen or her garden, and my father watching his cowboy movies when he is home.

I follow my mom into the kitchen. She has pulled a chair up to the counter to use as a stool to grab one of her many vases from the top cupboard.

"Is there anything I can do to help?" I asked her as I grabbed the chair to put away once she stepped off.

"Just tell your dad to turn the television off. Dinner is on the table," she informed me as she placed the arrangement on the kitchen island.

As we all gathered at the table, I saw that my mom had outdone herself yet again with hot lasagna cooling to the side, garlic bread fresh from the oven and homemade Caesar salad.

"This looks delicious, Mom!" I told her as I began to fill my plate.

"I just hope you like it. I wanted to spoil you a little bit, Wynne. You've had a lot on your plate and I'm sure you've been dealing with a lot of issues lately. I just wanted to take care of my little girl," Mom told me as she reached for my hand.

I looked at her. She was holding my hand and had a maternal look in her eyes. I then looked at my dad, and when he caught me looking at him he quickly glanced down at his plate.

"You told her, didn't you?" I asked my father.

My dad looked up at me and gave a shrug of his shoulders.

"Your father didn't have to tell me anything, Wynne. Do you honestly think I wouldn't have figured it out? It might have taken me a while, but a mother always knows her daughter's heart. I knew you were the one to call off the wedding. You were too calm and defensive of Jude to be the jilted bride. But yes, your father confirmed it this morning, and then Nancy called me this afternoon," my mom admitted to me while she continued to hold my hand.

"Mom," I sighed, "what did Nancy have to say when she called?" I should have known that this was more than a simple dinner invitation.

"Oh you know Nancy. It takes a lot for her to apologize, but she won't back down if she feels she has made a mistake. She just said that she was sorry for allowing something so trivial as our children's problems to get in the way of our friendship. I told her that as mothers our children always come first, and that our friendship never deteriorated, it was just on hiatus for awhile," Mom explained to me.

"So that means... what exactly?" I asked.

"Well, we are going out for coffee sometime next week. I'll let you know so you can reserve a table for us. Now, enough of all this nonsense; just enjoy your dinner," replied my mom as she patted my hand and focused on her food.

"But..." I began.

My father gave his famous "harrumph" before I could say anymore. That was his way of letting me know to leave things alone. Taking his advice, I enjoyed my food along with the knowledge that my mom had always been there for me even when I didn't realize it.

I helped my mom clean up the kitchen after dinner while dad went back to the living room to watch more of his Western shows. Mom and I worked silently beside each other, washing dishes and putting food away. I was trying to work up the courage to say something about what was casually mentioned at the table when my mom turned to me.

"Now, Wynne. I'm only going to say this once, and then we'll consider this whole topic closed, ok? It's taken you three long years to admit to your father and I what really happened that day in the church. I wish you had felt confident enough to come to us before now to tell us the truth. It hurt my heart to know that you didn't trust us enough with the truth. We would have supported you no matter what, Wynne. But as it was, you left us in the dark and let you father held a grudge against a man that didn't deserve it," Mom said to me. I started to apologize but she cut me off.

"Now, I figured out awhile ago that Jude wouldn't have left you that day if it weren't for something that was important. I knew you were still in love with Richard, and I also knew that you were not willing to admit that to yourself. I just wish you had come to me. Now, your Father and I have had long talks, many times actually, about all of this. He wouldn't believe me until he heard it from your mouth. I'm not saying this to make you feel guilty. I love you, Wynne. You are the daughter of my heart and my blood. I just want you to know that we are always here for you, no matter what! You are not alone, no matter how high you like to build the walls around your heart, Wynne."

I went over to her and gave her a big hug. By this time, both of us had tears streaming down our faces. Every once in a while it is nice to be reminded that I don't always have to be the grown-up, that I can be the daughter and just soak up my parents' love.

"You're right, Mom. I should have told you guys from the beginning. I was afraid of being a disappointment to you," I confessed to her.

"Oh, honey. When will you realize just how proud of you we are! You are such a gift from the Lord to us, and look at all that He has blessed you with! You will never be a disappointment to us," Mom told me as she held me by the shoulders.

"Now, it's time we put this all behind us, and celebrate with chocolate cake!" Mom declared to me loud enough so my father could hear.

"What are we celebrating?" Dad shouted back from the living room. I could hear the squeak of his chair as he stood up and began walking back to the kitchen.

"Life, love and new happiness," my mom declared to him as he walked into the kitchen and placed his arms around her waist.

"Any excuse is a good excuse, when it comes to chocolate," Dad declared with a twinkle in his eye. And people wonder whom I inherited my love for chocolate from!

Armed with chocolate cake and hazelnut flavored coffee, I sat down at the kitchen table and spread out all the details of the party tomorrow night. I brought my book with the cut outs of colors and decorations that I like, and I could hear my mom sigh as she looked at all my plans.

"How I ever brought up a daughter as organized as you are, I'll never know." My mom declared as she shook her head.

"Not everyone likes the 'fly by the seat of your pants' arrangement like you, Mom," I told her. My mom has a tendency to live her life with the assumption that everyone else knows exactly what she is thinking, and that everything will come together the way it should without too much effort on her part.

"Oh shush, you! I like what you have done, and it looks like you have all your ducks lined up in a row," she encouraged me as she perused all the information I had laid out for her to see.

"As long as everyone can help out in the way they agreed to, it should be fine," I said to her. This was a gentle reminder of her promises to help with desserts and to decorate the room in the church.

"I already have a crew set up to meet at the church Friday after lunch. Everything will be fine, Wynne!" Mom said as she walked over to her 'to do' board and began to read off the names of the ladies who would help to set up the room. I felt a sense of pride as I heard the Latte Ladies' names come up. I can always count on them to help me out.

Realizing just how late it has become and feeling reassured that at this point everything that I could have done is done, I thanked my mom for dinner and cake and prepared to leave. Armed with all my papers and a few Tupperware containers full of lasagna and chocolate cake, I was just about to walk out the door when my mom stopped me.

"Wynne, you won't forget about your date Friday night, will you?" she asked me somewhat hesitantly.

"No, Mom," I sighed, "I haven't forgotten. Can you have him just meet me at the church though? I plan on going over early," I asked her.

"At the church? I already gave him directions to your house, Wynne!" she whined to me while she wrung her hands. Oh-oh, not a good sign.

"Mom, meeting at my house just isn't going to work. Besides, I don't even know this man! I think I would feel more comfortable meeting him for the first time in a public place. Please, can you rearrange whatever plans you made for me?" I asked her.

My mom stood there for a few moments looking at the ceiling with a thoughtful look on her face. I could hear her muttering a little bit while she was trying to formulate a new plan.

"Actually, I think meeting at the church is a great idea!" she said to me.

"Great! I appreciate that, Mom. Please remember, though, that this date is only for one night—no other promises, Mom!" I reminded her.

"Oh I know, Wynne. No promises. But I don't really think that will be such a big deal once you meet him face to face," she said with an assurance to her voice that I'm not too sure if I really liked.

"Can you give me any hints at all about this mystery guy?" I asked her hopefully.

"Wouldn't you like to know!" she said giggling.

"I can see you'll be difficult! Thanks again for dinner, Mom. I love you!" I said to her as I gave her a quick hug goodbye.

"Good night, Wynne! Sweet dreams, honey," my mother said to me as she closed the door.

Sweet dreams! Wouldn't that be nice? I wonder if Richard has written me back. I certainly wouldn't mind dreaming about him tonight.

With that in mind, I suddenly remembered that I still had to respond to his email. He asked me about a dream I recently had. Do I dare tell him? Perhaps I can be a bit cryptic in my reply and let him read between the lines. I'm not sure if I want to bare my soul to him so soon in such a personal way.

155

Upon opening the door to my home I could immediately smell something burning. Oh no! Quickly walking towards my kitchen, I notice the smell becoming stronger. I can hear the kittens running around in the kitchen and I make a sudden stop at the doorway of my kitchen. I just cannot believe what I am seeing.

I must have forgotten to turn off my coffee machine, so that explains the burnt smell. But the mess that awaits me I can only blame on my two small housemates. Both flowerpots that were arranged on my kitchen counter had been knocked over, with soil all over the place. I can see tiny cat prints all through my kitchen from them walking through the dirt. The Tupperware container of muffins that I had left on the shelf obviously had not been closed tightly enough, and the kittens managed to figure out that if they knocked the container onto the floor, the lid would pop off and they could have a feast. Unfortunately, they haven't quite learnt to use a broom yet, and pieces of muffin are now ground into my kitchen rug and all over their faces. My cup of pens is knocked over, the neat pad of papers that I had beside my phone is no longer so tidy, and it appears that the knitted hand towel I had hanging from the oven door is now one long piece of thread that does not in any way resemble the towel it once was.

This is not the sight that I wanted to see when I came home. I had envisioned a quiet house filled with softly playing jazz music. I would listen to my phone messages and then spend some time on the computer. I would then grab a good book and settle into a warm cozy bed and relax before drifting off to sleep.

I certainly didn't think that I would be spending the next hour cleaning up my kitchen. Nor did I think that I would be too exhausted to even want to look at my computer once I had finished replanting my poor plants, winding up the ball of yarn that was all over my kitchen, vacuuming my kitchen rugs and then washing my floor to get rid of all the dirt marks. Yet, I wasn't willing to let the opportunity to write Rich back pass me by, so I gathered my laptop and sat on the couch, arranging myself so that I would be comfortable. Turning up my music just enough to have the relaxing feel of jazz swirl around me, I re-read Rich's email from earlier and thought about how I would answer.

> *To the curious Rich:*
> *So you want to hear about a dream. Would the one where I found myself dressed as a clown amidst a huge crowd of children suffice? Or how about when I found myself locked in a room filled with mountains of mouth watering chocolate?*
> *Or would you rather hear about a dream where I was standing on the shore with my feet in the water. The sound of the waves was romantic and I wasn't alone? Hmmm, maybe you'll just have to ask me in person :)*
> *Can I ask you a favor? Please give me advanced warning when you plan on surprising me. You know how much I hate surprises!*
> *It would be nice to actually talk to you. Do you think we could do that soon?*
> *Smiling, Wynne.*

I smiled as I re-read the message I wrote to him. I hope he smiles when he reads it. I hit send and was about to sign off when I decided to check my 'forums' to see if anyone had responded to my requests for product. I was pleasantly shocked at the amount of responses I received. Some were able to give me amounts immediately, and some still had some questions, which is normal amongst new clients. Close to an hour later I am done answering questions, paying amounts due and just answering general emails when a new message suddenly pops up.

Rich had written me back.

> *To the night-owl, Wynne;*
> *You don't play fair when it comes to your dreams. Just for that, no phone call before I arrive, but I will warn you that it will be soon, and at the exact moment that you are not expecting it. That should keep you on your toes for a little while!*

*I will be out of town for the next couple of days.
All work and no play make Rich a very boring boy.
Or so I've been told. I've been invited to stay with
some friends over the weekend, which live out of
town, so if you don't see a response from me before
then, that is why.*

*Behave yourself over the weekend, and eat some
chocolate for me (like that will be too difficult for
you!).*

Tired, but happy—Rich.

My initial reaction was sadness that I wouldn't be hearing
from him for a few days. Then I began to try to piece together
what exactly he said. He is going away and he would see me
soon. Would that mean that he is coming here this weekend to
see me? Susan and Matt wouldn't be the 'friends' he talked
about that invited him away. There's no way Susan could have
kept something that big of a secret from me. I immediately
thought of my mother and this 'mystery' date, but not even my
mother could pull this one off. My imagination is obviously
working overtime tonight, and I need to go to bed.

Knowing that there is no possible way of achieving sleep
anytime soon until this gets resolved, I quickly call Susan,
praying that she answers and not Matt.

"Hi there!" Susan greets me as she answers the phone.

"Oh, I'm glad it's you! I was a bit hesitant calling, thinking
you might be sleeping, and I would wake up Matt," I told her
with relief in my voice.

"Nope, I'm just finishing off those desserts I told you I
would make, and Matt is just watching TV. What's up?" she
asks me.

"I have a question for you and I'm hoping you'll be able to
answer," I told her.

"Ok, ask away!" she told me.

"You wouldn't by chance be involved with my mom in
setting me up with this 'mystery date' for Friday night, would
you?" I asked her.

"Why would I be involved in that? Your mom can play
matchmaker all by herself, she doesn't need my help," she
answered as I could hear the timer on her oven go off.

158

"Just a sec, Wynne," she said to me as she plopped the phone down on the counter. I could hear her in the background opening drawers, turning the buzzer off and then in the background I could hear her whispering to Matt.

"It's Wynne," I heard her whisper.

"Why is she calling this late?" I heard him ask in a normal tone.

"Shhhhh! She's on the phone! She's asking me about Friday." Susan whispered to him.

"Oh man, I'm going to bed!" he answered back, and then I could hear doors closing and Susan was back on the phone.

"Sorry about that. The squares were done and I didn't want them to burn," she said to me. Should I mention what I heard or just ignore it?

"Why were you just whispering to Matt?" I decided to just plunge in and ask her.

"What? Oh, yah, Matt was just heading off to bed," Susan answered a bit hesitantly.

"So why were you whispering?" I persisted.

"Um, the birds are sleeping. So what was it you asked me earlier?" she evasively asked me.

"Ok, I'll leave it alone. I asked you about this weekend and what plan you have concocted with my mother," I told her. Two can play at this game.

"Wynne, I'm not in cahoots with your mom on anything! I learned my lesson long ago that when you play with your mom, you always get burnt one way or another! Why, what's going on?" she asked me innocently. I'm not sure if I should believe her or not.

"Well, I just received an email from Richard tonight, and well, I think I just read too much into it." I conceded defeat.

"Oh, ok. Sorry I couldn't help you. It's late, and we have a busy day tomorrow," she said to me hastily before she hung up.

I just looked at the phone. I wasn't even given a chance to say good night. I'm not sure what is going on, but either I just caught her at a bad time, or she's in with my mom big time! She didn't even ask me what Rich said in the email! That's not like her at all.

I know that this whole evening's happenings, from dinner at my parents, to the email I received, and now this conversation with Susan, will play out in my head over and over and over again. So I head off with my book and have another hot bath. That should relax me enough so that when my head hits the pillow, I will go to sleep right away.

Or at least I hope that will happen.

I dream of chocolate
day & night.

Chapter 14

FRIDAY MORNING BEGAN WAY TOO EARLY for me. I was having such a sweet dream. It was a dream of pure romance. When Richard and I were dating in college, we would often come back here on the weekends and visit my parents. Just outside of town is a little park, complete with it's own stream. One day Rich decided that he wanted to teach me how to skip rocks. We had just started to date, and the newness of everything was so unique and special. Before we arrived we had stopped at the ice cream shop in town and bought a large sundae to split. I love chocolate and he wanted caramel, so we combined the two flavors together. There was a little bench in front of the stream where we sat and ate our sundae together, and then Rich showed me how to skip rocks. I can distinctly remember how it felt to have his arms around me, holding me close, trying to guide my hand in throwing the rock in just the right way onto the water. I never learned how to make it skip. Mine would just plop into the water, while his would glide across the water as if it were ice. We had so much fun, though; there is such innocence in the beginning of a relationship. That will always be a happy memory for me.

In my dream we were at this same spot sharing the same sundae. But instead of skipping rocks, Rich was declaring his undying love to me. We were standing by a tree that was close to the water. My back was against him, and he held me in his arms. It was a comfortable feeling, as if this was the place that I was meant to be. In my ear, Richard was professing his love, his commitment and his desire for us to be together. It was such a sweet romantic dream. That is, until my kittens decided it was time for me to wake up. One was at my ear licking it and the other managed to find my toe at the end of the bed and had decided it was a new toy. This was not the way that I wanted to end my dream.

Noticing the clock said 7:35 AM, I decided it was way too early for me to be up, and after nudging the kittens ever so gently to move and play elsewhere I rolled over to try to find my dream once again. Someone else had other plans, though. The phone began to ring.

"Good morning sweetheart," I heard my mother greet me.

"Hmmm. That depends Mom. Why are you calling me so early?" I mumbled to her. All I wanted to do was close my eyes and go back to la-la land.

"Wynne, dear. Wake up. I'm outside your door. Come open it, please. It's not exactly warm out today. I have coffee and bagels if that will help." My mother was trying to tempt me to get out of bed, and it was almost working.

"Coffee? Bagels? Hmmm, I'll be right there Mom," I tell her.

I make myself roll out of bed, hop around the floor trying to find my slippers and grab my robe as I walk out my bedroom door. I am not a morning person.

I can hear my mother banging on the door. I try to make my legs walk faster, but it is still too early so I shuffle across my hardwood floors until I reach the front door.

"Brrrr." I feel the wind hit me as I opened the door. When I look up I see not only my mother but also the rest of the Latte Ladies greeting me with huge smiles on their faces. They are all bundled up against the chilly winter wind, so I quickly reach for the coffee and bagels that my mom is holding in her hands and motion for everyone to come inside.

I led the way to my kitchen. On the way I call out to the ladies.

"Now, you know that if you had come this morning without coffee I would have barred all entry into my home, don't you?" I teased them as they followed me into the kitchen.

"Why do you think we brought coffee and bagels?" Judy said to me as she gave me a quick hug.

Judy McNeil, my second mother, knows me so well.

"I hope you don't mind that I joined your Latte group this morning, Wynne?" Mom said to me as she began to distribute the coffee around to the ladies.

"Not at all, Mom. You should join us more often," I encouraged her while I took the coffee that she handed me. Just feeling the heat of the coffee was enough to begin to wake my senses.

"Why are you all here so early, though?" I asked them all. "Weren't we meeting later this morning?"

Joan handed me a bagel to place in the toaster I had sitting on my cupboard.

"Honey, we have so much to do today, that we wanted to get an early start," Joan informed me.

I look around the room feeling like I'm missing something.

"What all do we have to do today that makes an early start so necessary?" I asked them. As far as I was concerned, the timetable was already set. A group of ladies would convene at the church around noon to begin decorating. Those who had to make desserts and finger food were either to bring their plates during this time or anytime after 5 PM when I had decided to be at the church overseeing any last minute details. That basically left the morning free, or so I thought.

This time Tracey spoke up.

"Wynne, you've had such a busy week, that we all decided that you needed a little pampering today. You have an appointment this morning at 9:30 AM at The Pampering Palace for a full morning of spa treatments. Then at lunch a few of us are taking you on a shopping trip to pick out a stunning dress for tonight. Once we find that dress, you have an appointment back at The Pampering Palace for a makeover and a style. You are going to look like you walked out of a magazine by the time tonight comes around," she told me while all the ladies began to giggle.

The Pampering Palace was the only spa place in town that offered all the necessities to make you feel like a newer, sexier you—or so the slogan boasts. The last time I was in there was the morning of my wedding three years ago. If you ever want to be pampered, that is the place to go. But why do I need to go there today? I posed this question to the ladies.

My mother was the one to respond.

"Wynne, we can't have your mystery date seeing you tonight looking like you just spent the week organizing the whole event. He needs to see you in the very best light, looking relaxed and stunning," my mom informed me while placing her hands on her hips.

"Mom, come on!" I said to her. "I'm not even going to have time for the guy tonight. I've told you that. Don't expect anything to come about, ok?" I pleaded with her. I really don't want her getting her hopes up only to have them dashed. Now that I've actually heard from Richard and know that there is a possibility to explore whatever is between us, I have no interest in getting to know anyone else.

"Wynne, just at least try! You can do that for me can't you?" she asked me.

I really didn't want to get into this with the other ladies around, so I just smiled and sighed. I think she took that as my acceptance cause she produced a huge smile and clapped her hands together in delight.

"Well, the past couple of days have literally flown by it seems," I said hesitantly while looking at all the ladies gazing at me with hope in their eyes.

"Who could pass up a day of pampering and being made to feel like a princess?" I asked them, feeling somewhat resigned. Amongst the squeals of delight that I accepted so easily, I could hear Judy whisper in my ear to enjoy the day and just rest in God.

After an early breakfast of coffee and bagels combined with laughter and fun, I managed to convince the ladies to leave me in peace to get ready for my spa treatment. Tracey stuck around; I don't think she quite believed that I would actually go. While I was getting ready, I could hear Tracey on the phone to Susan letting her know that I wouldn't be in the store today. I could hear a bunch of whispering, but since she was down the hall, I couldn't hear too much. Just a lot of whispering and giggling coming from Tracey's end.

I spent a few quiet moments doing my devotions. Even though I didn't have a lot of time, I still wanted to make sure that I began this day right with God. Feeling a sense of peace within my spirit I knew I was ready for anything that came my way today. I had originally thought that I would be so busy organizing this party that I wouldn't have time to soak it in and enjoy it. Obviously my friends know me too well. Deciding to just relax and let God take over, I settled in my heart that I wouldn't dwell on thoughts of the future; instead I would enjoy every aspect of this day. Even the part where my mom is trying to set me up on a blind date. I'll be polite and friendly, but I will try my best to make it known that there is no future for us. Just the knowledge that something could be happening between Richard and myself makes me want to smile. It wouldn't be fair of me to lead the poor sucker that my mom roped into becoming my blind date any further than necessary.

"Wynne!" Tracey was shouting at me. "What's taking you so long?" she asked while knocking on my bedroom door.

"I was just waiting for you to finish giggling with Susan on the phone. I didn't want to interrupt any secrets," I said to her with a wink.

"Gosh, no secrets—we were just talking about where to take you for your dress. Let's see, Value Village or The Bay. Such a hard choice!" she said teasingly.

"Oh, definitely Value Village! Why pay full price for an outfit you can get on sale!" I exclaimed while we both laughed.

"Come on, you. Let's get going," Tracey said as she pushed me out the door.

After a few hours of being treated like royalty, amongst the scrubbing and pounding massages, I began to actually feel like a princess. All this pampering can get to your head. Imagine sitting in a comfortable chair, getting a pedicure while you are sipping sparkling apple juice and having a plate of fruit and chocolate right at your fingertips. The only downfall is when you are receiving a manicure and you can't reach the delicious chocolate. Being pampered is a treat every woman should receive at least once in her life.

At exactly noon Susan and Tracey came into The Pampering Palace to escort me on a shopping trip. Going on a shopping trip with these two ladies is the experience of a lifetime. Tracey just lets herself go and experience the moment with no children involved, and Susan just loves to shop. Period.

After an exhausting two hours of trying on suits and dresses and mismatched outfits just for the fun of it, I finally managed to walk out of the store with not only a dress that we could all agree on, but a new pair of shoes and stockings to match. I have to admit that it is very seldom that I indulge and buy an honest-to-goodness dress. But this one just caught my eye and said 'pick me, pick me'. Now, how could I resist that?

When I walked out of the changing room wearing this particular dress, both Susan and Tracey just gasped. I spun around in front of the mirrors and I loved what I saw. An exotic black dress that had embroidered island-colored flowers flowing on the hem. The skirt of this dress swirled around my legs as I spun around. It had a scooped neckline that included a scarf in the same exotic colors that were on the skirt. The sleeves were three-quarter length with a small cuff at each end. I felt beautiful in this dress.

As I spun around in the dress I had the desire to live out my dream at least for one night. Why not pretend that I am single and free, that this night is just for me. How much harm would that be?

After walking out of the store with my purchases, we decided to stop at Starbucks for a Vanilla Bean Latte. This is an extra special treat, and no counting calories are allowed—that was declared the moment we all walked into the coffee shop.

We had just enough time to enjoy our lattes before I needed to be back at The Pampering Palace for the rest of my beauty treatment. The very thing that I was dreading this morning has become a treat that I am memorizing for future references. The three of us decided this was a gift that we would give to each other every year. We would create our own special chick day where we treat ourselves like princesses.

With the guarantee that Susan and Tracey would run over to the church to make sure everything was coming along as planned and then come back to not only report but to pick me up and help me get dressed, the two ladies left while I sank into the plush white chair and allowed the magic to transform me into a princess.

After two hours of fussing over my makeup and my hair I was declared ready. I was not allowed to look in the mirror the whole time. I know I received a new hair cut, and some new colors were applied to my face that I never thought I would wear, but as for the overall look, I had no idea what the effect would be until I could hear the gasps of Susan and Tracey as they walked back into The Pampering Palace.

"Oh my gosh, Wynne—where have you been hiding?" was Susan's response to my, "Well?"

Tracey was just as flabbergasted.

"Wow—you look, wow! Your date will have no clue what hit him!" she professed to me.

"So I look ok, then?" I asked them, still a bit hesitant.

"Wynne, you look amazing! Don't you see what the right hair cut and colors can do for you?" Susan asked me, amazed that I was still unsure as to how I looked.

"Actually, I haven't been allowed to look in a mirror since they began," I confessed.

"Then we had better hurry up and get you dressed so you can see the stunning beauty you are in the mirror," she told me. With that being said, Tracey came over to me, handed me my coat while Susan pushed me out the door.

I was able to catch little glimpses of myself by the reflection in the windows, but I didn't see the whole effect until I had my new dress on. WOW. I almost didn't recognize myself. My haircut was in a layered bob just below my chin, my eyes seemed accentuated and the colors used on my face looked so natural yet bold. I've never been a big fan of a lot of makeup—a little mascara here, some eyeliner there and of course some lipstick for color, but that's about it. But I have to admit that I am amazed at the transformation. Perhaps a little more effort on my part wouldn't hurt now and then.

I stepped out of my room and walked down the hallway. Standing before me were Susan and Tracey. The looks on their face said enough.

"WOW, Wynne! You look amazing! Your mystery guy tonight won't know what hit him!" Tracey exclaimed.

"Promise me something, Wynne?" began Susan. "Promise me that you will just soak in everything tonight and run in the moment?"

At first I looked at her oddly. Then I smiled.

"I promise!" I said to her. Right now, anything could happen to me and I would run with it! If Brad Pitt were to enter the church tonight and ask me on a date, I would definitely run with it!

I look at my watch and realize that it is after 5 PM. I had originally planned on being at the church by now to help with all the last minute preparations.

"Alright girlies!" I said, "the coach awaits," I called to them as I bundled up in my winter coat and prepared to leave.

Thank goodness the weather decided to cooperate. Even though it's wintertime, it is fairly mild out tonight, despite all the snow that we received this past week. Most of the snowfall has melted away, and you can see the sagging snowmen in the front yard drooping, some barely even standing anymore. No need to shovel the walkway, in fact, you could probably go for a stroll with a warm sweater, scarf and mittens tonight if you felt so inclined.

Susan had Christmas music playing in her vehicle. With all the Christmas lights sparkling from the trees and homes, you could definitely feel the spirit of Christmas. As the girls dropped me off at the church and then pulled away to get themselves ready for tonight, I decided to slowly walk up the walkway to the church. With the warm breeze blowing and snow on the ground, you could almost feel the magic in the air. I found myself whistling "Walking in a Winter Wonderland" and feeling at peace within in my heart. I couldn't stop myself from silently praising God for all His goodness in my life. I spread out my arms and did a little twirl on the sidewalk. With all the beauty surrounding me, I almost felt like God had created this night with me in mind.

"Thank you Father," I whispered, "for this wonderful blessing!"

As I stepped through the door of the church, I gasped. The site before me is that of an indoor winter palace! The ladies have done such an amazing job!

The moment you walk into the church you feel like you have been transported to a winter getaway. A Christmas tree stands alone in the corner sparkling with lights and cranberries gracing the tree. There is a small table with candles glowing and a beautifully decorated book for guests to sign and write precious words of wisdom for the couple to treasure for years to come. There is a little bench beside the tree for women to sit and exchange their boots for shoes if they desire, and one of the youth of the church is standing beside the coat rack offering to hang coats for those just walking in. The lights have been turned down low so the only glow is from the Christmas lights on the ceiling as well as the tree, and the dozen candles that are blazing throughout the room.

To reach the downstairs you walk down a winding staircase. Normally the walls of the staircase are decorated with posters for Children's Church and various mission projects that the Sunday classes have taken on. Tonight though, these posters have been taken down and replaced with various printed frames portraying elegance and delicacy. One picture is of a snowflake; the other is of an outdoor winter scene. There is a large picture in the middle with white embossed paper and a gold ribbon as the only source of decoration on that frame. Winding its way down the stairs are even more soft white Christmas lights. When you reach downstairs, currently the door is closed, obstructing the view of the inside. Before the closed door is another Christmas tree that is decorated this time with white lights and gold ribbon. Simple, yet elegant in appearance.

As I open the door the signs of busyness excite me. Various ladies from the church are there creating the final touches to the décor in the room. When I mentioned that I wanted elegant, that is exactly what I received. I stop just inside the door and take a good look around the room. My mom is holding court over in the far corner. From what I can see, she is the one in charge here—good job Mom! I give her a quick wave and then the thumbs up sign, all the while she continues to stare at me.

All around the room are round tables that will each seat between six to eight people. They are in a circular design with a main round table in the middle. All the tables, save the middle one, are dressed in black and gold. There is a black tablecloth draping each table with a shorter gold cloth on top of this. Each place setting has a black charger plate with a white and gold rimmed plate above that. For centerpieces there are various candle displays on each table. The middle table is the accenting table. Stacey loves pink and somehow wanted this color incorporated into the design. Since Stacey and Jude will be sitting at the middle table, the underlining skirt is a deep rose color with a shorter gold color cloth on top of that. Their charger plates are gold with white plates rimmed with a bold black strip. For the centerpiece of their table there is a vase that has been filled with water and pink sparkles. Floating candles are inside the vase and arranged around the vase are pink colored votives. Just perfect!

As you walk into the room, beside the door is another Christmas tree. This one is decorated with white sparkling lights and white and pink ribbon and strings. Christmas lights are strung on the ceiling and thick tube-like lights outline the room on the floor. Soft instrumental music is being played in the background. The ladies are adding the final touches to each table, and I can see ladies in the kitchen arranging various dishes of desserts. There is a long table against one wall that is decorated in pink and gold. I'm assuming this will be the table for the desserts and punch. Beside the tree is a table in the same colors with wrapped gifts already on top.

As I stand there Judy and Pastor Joy from the Latte Ladies come up to me to give me hugs. They look like they are on their way out.

"Wynne, you look amazing! A fairytale princess come true," gushes Pastor Joy to me while admiring my dress.

"Looks like a day of pampering suits you! You look beautiful," admired Judy as she stood back to get a good look at the overall effect.

"Thanks! I had so much fun, thank you so much for doing this for me!" I thanked them as I gave each lady a hug.

"This place looks fantastic!" I told them.

"You have your mother to thank for that. She made sure that all your ideas were workable and that we could all help to create this dream," Pastor Joy informed me.

"Now we have to be off and get ready ourselves! Have fun, and we'll see you soon!" Judy told me as they continued to walk out the door.

After they left, I walked over to my mom and gave her a hug.

"Thank you so much, Mom! This looks perfect!" I told her. I'm still amazed at how it all came together.

"This is an important night, Wynne, I just wanted to make it perfect for you!" Mom replied as she hugged me back. I could see tears in her eyes.

"Wynne, you look so beautiful!" Mom cried as she gazed at me.

"Well, I know I look good, but why is it so shocking to everyone?" I asked her. The reaction of everyone so far is leaving me with a weird feeling. Do I normally not look good; so that when I do dress up, the change is so startling that everyone notices?

My mom reaches up and pats my cheeks.

"Honey, your whole focus has been on your business and your home, that you have forgotten to focus on yourself! So yes, the change in you tonight is so evident that everyone will notice! Don't be ashamed, just reach out and grab onto life the way God wants you to!" she said to me encouragingly.

I smiled at her and knew that I had a twinkle in my eyes.

"I plan to, Mom, I plan to!" I said to her.

"Good," she replied. "Now go and grab an apron and help out in the kitchen! Make sure it's a full apron though; I don't want you to get your dress dirty! If you had listened to me in the first place, this wouldn't even be an issue!" she said to me as she tried to scoot me towards the kitchen.

"Mom, if I had listened to you, then I would still be at home getting ready while you were here directing. Nope. It's time for you to go home now and get ready. Dad promised me he would come tonight." I said to her as I took the clipboard that she was holding from her hand and walked her to the door.

With only an hour left before everyone would begin to arrive, I made a quick sweep of the list my mom created to see what else needed to be done. Noticing that everything had been checked off, I decided to go into the kitchen to see how I could help there. The moment I walked into the kitchen Joan was there with an apron to put on. I just laughed and told her all mothers think alike.

"No honey—this is a woman thing, not a mother thing! What woman in her right mind would want to get all messy after she has just spent a day of pampering and looks absolutely gorgeous?" she asked me with a southern twang to her voice.

I laughed at her and began to work on a tray of goodies.

Chocolate creates
Romantic Adventures.

Chapter 15

AN HOUR INTO THE PARTY, I KNEW it was a success. Jude and Stacey arrived a few minutes early and they made the exact same movements that I made when I first walked in. I made sure I was at the front door to greet them when they arrived. Jude looked around and made an average male comment.

"Very nice," he said while shrugging off his jacket and taking Stacey's wrap.

Thankfully Stacey had a completely different reaction. The moment she walked into the front entrance she was enthralled. You could tell by the look in her eyes that this was exactly what she had envisioned.

"Oh, Wynne! This is amazing! It's gorgeous!" she gushed as she looked around.

"Just wait, Stacey, until you see the downstairs," I warned her.

"Oh I can't wait! Come on Jude!" she cried as she tugged at his hand.

I followed them down the stairs and soaked in all the comments Stacey made on her way down. Although I didn't personally create the atmosphere here tonight, I felt so proud of the ladies who did.

Just as we reached the bottom of the stairs I called to Jude and asked him to wait. I gave Stacey a moment to gather her thoughts. I wanted to share something that was on my heart with them, but I didn't want Stacey to be completely focused on the decorations that she lost what I had to say.

"Jude, tonight is such a special night for you and Stacey. There were so many ladies that came today to help make this whole night a possibility. There will be time tonight for you both to have a few words. Could you make sure that you give them all the credit and not me?" I asked him. If I remember correctly, Jude has a habit of not thinking before speaking and I

177

wanted to make sure that he didn't end up sticking both feet in his mouth tonight.

"Of course, Wynne. I know how much you hate having the spotlight on yourself. Don't worry. Even though I know you were the mastermind behind tonight, I'll place all the glory on the other ladies," Jude informed me.

"No, that's not what I meant. Jude, Stacey—the moment I made the decision to throw this party for you, I had so many ladies rally around me concerned that I was doing this for all the wrong reasons. So they decided, all on their own, I might add, to throw this party for you instead, as a group. Basically all the ladies who helped to raise you in this church are the ones who are showering their love on you tonight! I just had the idea, but they made that idea their own," I told him a little desperately. I wanted to make sure that they understood what tonight was all about.

Stacey took hold of my hands.

"Wynne, we completely understand! This will be a night where we will always remember that this church showered love upon us," Stacey confirmed exactly what I was hoping to hear.

"Thank you, Stacey! This night is for you guys, and I hope that you will enjoy it! I am so happy for you both!" I told them as I began to open the door to the main room.

Inside, the majority of those who were coming had already shown up. Everyone was waiting for the guests of honor to arrive. Pastor Joy offered to host the evening for me, so that I could be free to focus on my date tonight, she informed me a few days ago. So once I walked the newly engaged couple into the room, I was free to melt into the crowd and wait for my mystery date to arrive.

The moment Jude and Stacey walked into the room everyone began to clap. I made sure that I hung back a little bit; giving the couple enough time to walk into the room and begin to mingle. I could hear Stacey exclaim over how beautiful the room looked. I smiled, knowing that this will be a night she will always remember.

I guess I waited too long because just as I was about to enter Susan came walking out the door looking for me.

"What are you doing out here by yourself? Waiting for your date?" she asked me as she took my hand.

"No. I'm sure my mom will find me when he arrives. I was just wanting to give them some time to get in before I followed them," I told her. In all honesty, I hadn't thought about my mystery date too much tonight. I thought I would leave the introductions up to my mom whenever he decided to arrive.

"Well, come on then. You don't want people to begin to wonder where you are, do you?" she asked me as she tugged me into the room.

"I hope you saved me a seat," I said to her as we wove our way through the crowd trying to talk to Jude and Stacey.

"Of course I saved you a seat! I'm offended! What kind of friend would I be to leave you on your own with a mystery guy?" she asked me with a shocked look on her face.

"Hmm, that is true! As if you could really leave me alone with the guy before you found out all there is to know about him!" I teased her as we found our seats and sat.

"You know her too well!" confirmed Matt as he overheard our conversation. Stacey just grinned, not at all embarrassed that we figured out her true intentions.

"So where is this mystery man?" Matt asked me as he looked about.

"The way I figure there are two reasons why he's not here yet. One, my mother gave him her famous directions and he's now on the other side of town completely lost, or two, his sanity returned and he realized what a horrible idea this was!" I said to him as I smiled.

Both Matt and Susan laughed. My mother and her sense of directions are famous around here. You only have to experience the sense of becoming lost once before you figure out that to go the opposite way that she told you is the right way. I can't tell you how many times growing up we got lost on trips, all thanks to my mom who would insist on taking care of the map. When my mom tells you to turn left, you turn right; when she tells you that it's just down the road a bit, be prepared for a long drive.

"I would bank on the fact that he got turned around," Matt told me. "Any guy who would turn down a date with you tonight needs to be in a mental hospital!"

"Doesn't she look fantastic tonight?" Susan reiterated for the millionth time. I know she's just trying to boost up my self-esteem, but enough already!

"Alright, alright! Enough Susan! If I have one more person tell me how gorgeous I look tonight, I'll scream!" I said in mock anger.

"Just soak it up, will you? No woman in their right mind would deny a compliment when she deserves it!" Susan said to me.

I stood up to go look at all the presents at the gift table. I was beginning to feel a bit antsy, and I just needed to move around.

"I'm not denying it, Susan. I just don't need to hear it anymore." I tossed my hair over my shoulder as I walked away from her.

About an hour into the party, I was beginning to feel like I had been stood up. By now all the guests had arrived and the majority of the food had been eaten. Stacey is in the middle of opening the numerous gifts that they received while Jude is sitting there fiddling with his drink looking completely bored. I was still feeling quite antsy and was constantly moving around.

I found myself continually watching the door. Every time I glanced that way, I would look at my parents who were sitting closest to the door. My mom would give me a look that meant 'be patient,' and my dad would just pat my mother's hand and give me a wink. Do they know something I don't?

I walked over to my parents' table. There was an empty seat beside my mother that was right in front of the door, so I sat there and turned towards her.

"Now be patient, dear. I know he's a little late, but he will be here," Mom said to me as she patted my hand. What is with her and patting my hand? Not only am I feeling a bit antsy, but I'm also starting to feel a bit grumpy.

"Mom, he's an hour late. It's quite obvious that he won't be coming, whoever he is. Thanks for the thought, though, I do appreciate it," I told her.

"He'll be here, honey," my dad interjected.

"Well, I'm glad that you both feel positive about this. I don't even know the guy, but if he has enough bad manners to not show up on a date, then I'm fairly certain that I don't want to waste my time getting to know him," I reasoned.

"Wynne, be patient dear! Now, why don't you go grab your mother a fresh cup of punch and something to munch on? Preferably chocolate if there is any left," she asked me, or rather, told me.

I walked over to see what types of goodies were on the table. There wasn't much of a selection left, even though the night was only half over. Making a mental note to go into the kitchen to see if there are any plates to bring out, I filled my mom's punch glass and placed it on the table while I glanced through the remaining selections of dessert. I chose a piece of chocolate brownie and a pecan tart for my mom and placed it on her plate. I was just about to take the final piece of cheesecake for myself when from behind me I could hear my name being called. Thinking that maybe my date had finally arrived, I turned around and suddenly felt my plate slip from my hand.

There, standing before me, was my date.

I began to visibly shake. I stood there in complete shock and could not form a single thought, let alone a word.

He just stood there. There was a gentle smile on his face along with a questioning look in his eyes.

I found myself unable to do anything but stare.

"This is where you are supposed to say hello," he said to me softly.

Hello? Hello? How in the world can I even imagine saying 'hello' when I'm finding it difficult to comprehend the very fact that he is standing before me with a bouquet of roses in his hand and a smile on his face?

"Ok, well, how about 'am I dreaming' if you can't say hello," he continued. He had one of those earth-shattering lazy smiles on his face. I can tell he loves my response.

I find myself beginning to smile.

"Am I dreaming?" I asked him teasingly. Everything else has faded to the background. The only person in my reality at this moment is the one standing before me.

"Richard?" I asked hesitantly. I felt in my heart I knew the answer of why he was here, but I still needed to ask. "Why are you here?"

Richard took a step, coming closer to me. His eyes spoke volumes, but it was the words that he spoke that I so desperately needed to hear.

"I've come to make your dreams come true, Wynne," he whispered to me softly.

I felt so lost in the moment. Everything in my heart screamed 'YES!' and I felt my body respond in the same manner.

"You are my dream come true," I whispered back to him as I closed the space between us. I raised my hands to his face. I felt I needed to physically touch him in order to convince myself that he was really here and not just a dream.

I closed my eyes when my hand rested on his face. I heard him whisper my name. I wanted, no, I needed to soak in this moment, a moment that was actually real and not just a dream.

I opened my eyes and smiled.

"Hi," I whispered.

With that, Rich's eyes lit up and he laughed.

As I began to laugh with him, I looked around and realized that we were being watched. I reached out my hand towards Richard. He looked at me and slowly brought his hand forward.

"I'm Wynne," I introduced myself. "You must be my mystery date," I said to him with laughter in my voice.

It took Rich a moment to grasp what I was doing, but once he realized that we had an audience, he slowly shook my hand.

"Wynne, what a beautiful name for such a beautiful lady," he began.

"My name is Rich, and yes, I'm your mystery man. I hope you don't mind that I brought you some roses," he said to me as he handed me the beautiful bouquet.

While our hands were intertwined together, my mother walked over to my side.

"I see you've solved the mystery," she said to me as she placed her arm around my waist.

I just looked at her. Solved the mystery? What did she mean?

Richard saw the look I gave my mom and gave a short laugh.

"You mean, you never figured it out?" he said to me in disbelief. "Didn't I leave enough clues for you?" he asked, as he looked first at my mother and then at myself.

"Clues?" I asked him while feeling a little bit out of my league.

My mother just laughed.

"Oh, Wynne. Rich felt so bad that he insisted on giving you hints of this instead of just showing up without any warning," Mom explained to me.

"I know how much you hate being left in the dark, and I remember quite clearly how you react to surprises, so I wanted to make sure that I gave you plenty of time to get used to the idea that I wanted back in your life," Richard continued the explanation my mother had started.

I began to clue in just as Susan and Matt walked over to us.

Susan gave Richard a big hug, and introduced her husband Matt to him. The boys shook hands before Susan turned to me with a smile on her face.

"Do you have any idea how difficult this was to keep as a secret?" she asked me.

"You knew!" I accused her while wagging my finger in her face. "How could you know about this and not tell me?" I asked her.

"You have no idea how hard it was for her, Wynne!" Matt told me while placing his arms around his wife.

"Seriously, you have no idea!" Susan agreed while she nestled in his arms.

"Do you have any idea how many times I had to stop myself from giving you hints?" she asked me.

I wasn't about to let them all off this easily.

"So what about the time we went out to Mama Roses' for dinner? If it was such a secret, why did you tell me you had been in touch with Rich?" I demanded.

Richard answered before Susan had the chance to.

"I was the one who asked her to do that," he admitted. "I wanted you to start thinking about having me back in your life, and I knew Susan was the perfect person to get you thinking," he told me.

My mother turned to me.

"Honey, you're not upset with us, are you?" she asked.

"How exactly do you fit into this picture, Mom?" I responded in turn with a question of my own.

Again Richard was the one to provide the answer to my question.

"After Susan gave me the heads up that you were becoming more receptive to the thought of having me back in your life, I decided to get in touch with your mom and see if she could help me," he explained.

"Such perfect timing!" My mother jumped in. "He called right after Nancy informed me about tonight's party, and you know me, I got the great idea of him coming tonight as your guest," Mom continued.

"Hmm, so basically, you all knew about this and just left me in the dark," I said to them. I found myself feeling a mixture of hurt that they would keep this from me, but also a bit of happiness that they would actually do this for me as well.

At that moment, when everyone was silent, trying to figure out a way to get out of the situation they placed themselves in, Tracey walked up.

"You made it!" Tracey loudly exclaimed while she threw her arms around Rich and gave him a hug.

This captured the attention of all the others in the room that hadn't previously noticed us, and I could hear things begin to quiet down as we were being observed.

Richard placed his hands on Tracey's shoulders and stood back from her.

"Look at you!" he said. "Mother of three, a pastor's wife, and you still look as lovely as ever!" Rich complimented her while Pastor Mike, her husband, walked over.

"Hey man! Long time no see," greeted Mike warmly. Richard and Mike had become friends while we were all together in school.

I was starting to feel a bit awkward just standing there while being ignored by one set of friends and being watched by those still seated at their tables around the room.

"Ahem," I called out. "I do believe that this is *my* mystery date," I pouted. I looked over at Richard and found him smiling at me.

"Would you be greatly offended if I whisked you away tonight, Wynne?" he asked me while the others just looked on and smiled.

"Well, I really should stick around to help clean up," I said hesitantly.

"Nonsense!" my mother spoke up, just as I was hoping she would. "You go on, Wynne, just leave the clean up to me," she said to me as she pushed me towards Richard.

Just as Rich reached out to grasp my hand, Mike spoke up. "We'll leave the door unlocked for you, Rich."

I looked up at Rich with a question in my eyes.

"Didn't you read my email?" he asked me. "Some friends invited me to spend the weekend with them," he explained with a grin.

I looked over at Tracey and just smiled. She gave me a big hug and whispered in my ear.

"Make your dreams become reality, Wynne."

I closed my eyes, took a deep breath and began to walk with Richard towards the door. When I had enough nerve, I glanced up at him, only to find him smiling down at me.

"I am so glad that you are really here!" I said to him.

"I've waited a long time to hear you say that, Wynne," Rich said to me with a sparkle in his eyes.

We had just finished walking through the doorway and were about to begin walking up the stairs when we heard someone come walking quickly behind us.

It was Jude. He had a different sort of look in his eyes. Almost as if he knew immediately that this was the man who had claimed my heart so long ago.

Richard steadily looked at Jude as he walked towards us. I could feel a slight tightening of his hand as he held mine. When I looked at him, he seemed to stand a bit taller and had a determined look on his face.

Jude, on the other hand, seemed to have his shoulders stooped as he stood there looking up at Richard. The tension between the two men was quickly mounting.

"Jude, I'd like you to meet Richard. Richard, this is Jude. Tonight's party is to celebrate his new engagement with the beautiful lady standing right behind him," I said nervously as I introduced the two and saw Stacey standing in the background watching the exchange.

Both of the men nodded their heads at each other while they shook hands.

Stacey walked up to Jude and placed her arm around his waist.

Richard then placed his arm around my shoulders.

"Well," I said trying to break the tension. I cocked my head to the side and looked at Stacey.

"I hope you don't mind that I am leaving early," I said to her.

"Not at all!" she replied with a smile. "Thank you so much for everything! You go and have an awesome evening. You deserve it," she said to me. I could tell that she meant it.

I looked at Jude and gave him a smile. I watched him as he looked from me to Richard and then back at me again.

"Nice meeting you, Jude," Richard said. "Congratulations and I pray that you find happiness together."

"Goodnight," I called out as Rich and I began to walk up the stairs.

"So that was the man I thought had taken you away from me," Richard said quietly as we walked up.

"That was the man who refused to become second best," I said to him as I squeezed his hand.

"Hmmm," was all he said as he helped me into my jacket.

Richard walked me down the walkway. When we were half way down he stopped and looked up to the sky.

"It's such a beautiful night, a night of new beginnings," I said to him.

He looked down at me with such a tender look in his eyes.

"What are you thinking?" I asked him.

He stood there silently for a moment while looking deep into my eyes.

"I was just thanking God that He is the God of second chances."

There was nothing that I could say to that. It was the perfect description of what was beginning to happen between us.

I turned to face him. Looking up into his eyes, I couldn't help but show my emotions to him. I could feel tears begin to well up. He quietly brought me to him in a gentle hug. It felt so good to be held in his arms. I took a deep sigh, breathing in the very essence of him. He placed his cheek against the top of my head.

"Do you feel it?" He whispered to me as I stood there in his arms.

"The peace?" I asked him.

"Knowing that this is the place where you belong, in my arms," he responded.

I began to shiver. Thinking I was cold, Rich gently withdrew from the hug and began to lead me toward his vehicle.

After climbing into his black Ford Escape, Richard quickly put the heat on and we sat there waiting for the vehicle to warm up.

"I wasn't cold, you know," I said to him.

"No?" he asked me giving me a strong look.

I just blushed and looked out the window, trying to gather my thoughts.

When I felt composed enough to face him, I turned and had a mischievous look in my eyes.

"So, since this is officially classified as a date... do you have any ideas of what we should do tonight?" I asked him.

"Hmm, I have some thoughts," he responded with the exact same look in his eyes that I had in mine.

"Can I ask what they are?" I ventured.

He just gave a chuckle.

"I had originally thought of taking you to the park where we used to skip rocks, but since it's the middle of winter, that won't do. Then I thought of going to a coffee shop where we could sit and chat, but then I realized that if I was to be honest, I just want to spend some time with you alone, not surrounded by other people," he said to me.

"Would you consider two kittens an invasion of privacy?" I asked him, forming a plan in my head.

"Would these kittens insist on sharing some of the pasta and dessert I picked up from Mama Rose's?" he asked me with a smile.

"You went to Mama Rose's already?" I asked him squinting my eyes.

"Why do you think it took me so long to get here tonight?" he answered. "She recognized me the moment I walked in and held me hostage for over an hour before allowing me to leave with enough food to feed an army!" he held his hands up in mock surrender.

Knowing Mama Rose, I can picture this clearly in my mind! That is exactly what she would do, not caring that she was holding him up or that I would be impatiently waiting for him at the church tonight. Of course, I had no idea he was my mystery date, but still.

I began to giggle.

"So what did she make you leave with? Please tell me there is a piece of cheesecake in there!" I begged him.

"A piece? Oh come on Wynne! There's a whole cake just for us! Including some delicious pasta, garlic bread and salad. She even placed an extra surprise in the bag, one she knew you would like," he told me with a hint of suspense in his voice.

"Oh, let me guess! Knowing Mama Rose, she probably placed some candles in the bag to add to the romance," I suggested to him.

Rich just winked at me as he drove out of the church parking lot.

I gave him directions to my house. I was feeling a bit nervous with him coming in. I knew that I didn't have time to clean up my house yet, and the mess in the kitchen from this morning when the ladies brought breakfast over to the house was still there.

When we pulled up in front of my home, there were little jars filled with candles lining the sidewalk up to my door. I looked over at Richard and he just smiled and shrugged as he stepped out of his door to walk around the vehicle to open my door.

"Don't ask," he said, "just enjoy."

I was rapidly trying to think of who would have come over to do this when Richard reached into his pocket and pulled out a key. When he inserted that key into the door to unlock it, I was about to ask him where he got the key when he placed his finger on my lips and said, "Shush."

The moment I walked into my front hallway I saw that someone had already thought ahead and prepared my home for our romantic date. My house was not only spotless, but there was a soft glow coming from the living room and dining room, and I could even see the soft flickering of candlelight coming from the kitchen. I could hear the kittens quietly meowing and assumed that whoever had come over tonight also placed the kittens in my bedroom.

Taking off our coats and shoes, Richard took my hand and led me through my living room and into the dining room. The table had already been set with my grandmother's china, candles lit and even more flowers filled the room than the bouquet that I held in my hands.

"This is beautiful!" I said to him as I took in all the candles and flowers.

"Why don't you place those flowers in a vase? The dinner has been placed in the oven on low to keep it warm." He informed me.

I smiled at him and felt so content.

"How did you do all this?" I asked him as I walked over and gave him a hug.

"Actually, Tracey and Mike were the ones to do this. They came over here and met me as I brought the food. Tracey placed our meal in the oven to keep warm, set the table and even placed all the candles on your walkway before we left. Mike helped me to light all the candles, and then just before we left Tracey locked your kittens in your room. I hope you don't mind?" he asked me somewhat hesitantly.

"Not at all," I responded to him feeling somewhat surprised. How like Tracey to do this. I'll have to make sure I thank her properly later.

We spent the majority of our time at the table trying to catch up on little things. I think we both decided to just go with the moment, to just enjoy what was going on for right now.

After enjoying a delicious meal, being surrounded by candlelight and feeling like I'm living in a dream, I offer to make some coffee and invite Richard to sit in the living room. It has been such a long time, and while it would be so easy to allow the romance of the evening to sweep us away, it is time to touch the ground, even for a moment, and talk about what is happening.

I brought out cups of hazelnut flavored coffee and found Rich to be sitting on the couch. He patted the cushion beside him, and after placing the cups of coffee down on the table in front of the couch I joined him.

There was a little bit of an awkward moment that developed. Rich decided to be the first to breach the moment.

"So that was Jude," he said. A mute point since I had introduced him earlier this evening, but it was the only way to bring up the subject neither one of us really wanted to discuss. At least I knew I definitely didn't want to discuss it. I'd much rather sink into his arms and tell him about the dreams I have been having the past year or so.

"That was Jude," I responded.

"For three years I thought you were off limits, a married woman. Do you know that I came to see you the day you got married, or at least the day I thought you were to be married?" he asked me.

I sat up straight and looked at him.

"I had no idea Rich! Where were you? What happened?" I asked him. A part of my heart sank.

"From the day you walked away from me, Wynne, I couldn't stop thinking about you. I prayed for you continually. I really believed that you were the woman that God created to make me complete. I knew you needed some time, so I gave you time. After two years I couldn't take it anymore. I felt an urgency to come and see you. I had it all planned. I would buy you roses; declare my undying love to you and we would live happily ever after. I felt so good about it. I arrived into town and stopped at the florist to buy you roses. When I walked into the store you should have seen the bouquets being arranged. The lady was on the phone so I found a bouquet that I liked and walked up to the counter. I could hear the woman talking about a wedding that was to start in an hour. I thought I heard your name, but I wasn't sure. Then I looked down, and there on the counter was your wedding invitation. I thought for sure I read it wrong, so I grabbed the paper and was reading it. The woman got off the phone and asked if she could help me. When I asked her about what I held in my hand, she seemed so happy for you. I was in shock, Wynne. I couldn't believe it," Richard explained to me. He reached out and grabbed his coffee. I stayed silent, knowing that he needed to finish.

"I rushed over to the church and I saw the parking lot full of vehicles and people walking around all dressed up. I walked into the church and saw your guest book. With your name and his name. My heart broke into little pieces, Wynne. I think that was the lowest point of my life. Up till then I had always felt so sure that you were the perfect woman for me, and that God would eventually bring us together. On that day all my dreams were destroyed," Rich whispered.

I looked at him and saw that he had tears in his eyes. We were both silently crying. I reached over and grabbed his hand. He began to rub my hand with his thumb. A very comforting feeling.

"I went home and decided to start a new life. I felt betrayed by God, and it took me a long time to deal with that. Forgiving God is very hard, I found that out the hard way. But forgiving ourselves for allowing our hearts to lose trust in God is even worse. Every once in a while I would talk to Tracey and Mike, but after that day I made them promise never to mention your name to me. I had to completely cut you off from my life. But that never works, does it? Do you have any idea what it is like to feel guilty for finding your thoughts automatically dwelling on a woman you thought was married for the past three years?" he asked me in anguish. My heart was breaking while listening to his story.

"Oh, Rich. I'm so sorry!" I said to him. That was barely enough, but I couldn't say anything else.

"Wynne, don't ever apologize. If I hadn't been stubborn, I would have found out the truth a long time ago," he told me with a sigh.

"So how did you find out that I never was married?" I asked him.

"Susan," he responded. "I ran into her one day, quite by accident, and before I could stop myself I found myself asking her about you," he told me.

"You wouldn't believe the shock I felt when she told me that you had started a store with her and her husband and that you were still single," he confessed.

191

"Believe me, Richard, when I tell you that I can imagine!" I told him, remembering how I felt when Susan told me that he wasn't married like I thought he must have been.

"Well," he said. "It was finding out that you were still single, and that you in fact never did get married that made me start to believe that my dreams weren't destroyed, that there was still some hope," he confessed to me.

"The rest you heard tonight at the church," he told me somewhat sheepishly.

I breathed a deep sigh and then smiled.

"Rich, I couldn't get married that day. Jude always knew that you held a large part of my heart, and that he would always be second best in my life and in my heart. Probably at the same time that you came to the church, Jude came into the room where I was and asked me if I could ever give him my whole heart. When I told him that I would never be able to do that, we both decided that it wouldn't be right to settle for second best. You were the only man who has ever or will ever own my heart, Richard," I softly told him. I waited breathlessly for his response.

Richard just looked at me with a strong gaze. It was if he was trying to look into the very soul of who I am. I looked back at him, hoping that he would be able to see the promise of love and a future in my eyes.

"Tell me about your dreams, Wynne," Richard asked me.

So for the next hour I proceeded to tell him about my dreams. Both the ones where I dreamt of him, and the ones that I had for my future plans. It was the perfect evening.

Realizing how late it was becoming, we made plans for the following day to spend together. Now that we were finally together and the thought of a future was before us, we wanted to spend as much time together as we could.

I walked Richard to the doorway. We both stood there together and stared into each other's eyes. Richard pulled me closer to him and held me against his heart. I could hear the rhythm of his heart beating.

I looked up into his eyes. I thought he was going to kiss me, but instead he placed a finger against my lips.

"Wynne. There is something between us that has never gone away and it never will. It is a gift from God that we have to accept. I love you. I have always loved you and I always will love you. I want to ask you a question that I want you to pray about. Please don't answer me now, just think about it. I don't want to live another day without you in my life. I want you to be the other half of me, I need you to complete me. Please, Wynne, become my wife and fill that empty space in my heart that was created just for you!" Richard pleaded with me with love shining through his eyes.

Before I could even answer him he lowered his mouth and kissed me.

It was the type of kiss that made all those kisses in my dreams fade away. It was even better than my dreams. This kiss spoke of love, commitment and promise.

Tears began to fill my eyes and fall down my face. Richard gently kissed those tears away and then whispered in my ear.

"Sweet dreams, my darling!"

6 months later...

Postlude

WE WERE SEATED ON THE BENCH by the tree sharing a sundae together. He was eating all the caramel sauce while I was digging for the hot fudge. We had just finished doing our devotions together, a habit we developed after the night of our mystery date. Whether we were online together, on the phone or in person, we would do daily devotions that only helped to strengthen our relationship.

Rich had come up for the weekend. School was now over for him and he had given his resignation to the school. This was his first weekend school-free, and he wanted to enjoy it to the fullest.

With the warm weather upon us we decided to head to the park, our favorite place, and enjoy the sunshine. Of course we had to share a sundae.

The past six months have been wonderful. Richard and I have become so close to each other. We have redefined our relationship by getting to know each other all over again. So many things happened within the five-year period that shaped who we have become. It has been fun, though, discovering each other's little quirks.

While Richard had plans to only relax and enjoy this weekend, I had decided to rock his boat a little bit. Six months ago he asked me a question that he wouldn't let me answer. It has never come up since then in words, but the thoughts and promise have always lingered between us.

With only half of the sundae left, I turned to Richard and gave him a kiss. He tasted like caramel and ice cream. Deliciously sweet and tempting.

"Richard," I began, "you asked me a question six months ago that you wouldn't let me answer at the time," I said to him.

Licking some caramel sauce off of his plastic spoon, he grinned.

"I did?" he asked me somewhat playfully. I swatted him on the arm.

"You did," I answered. "I have an answer for you, but I think you need to ask it to me it again," I told him with a little bit of prima donna attitude to my voice.

Rich had this mischievous look enter in his eyes when he answered me.

"Hmmm," he said thoughtfully, "I think you might need to refresh my memory some. Six months is a long time to remember something," he said to me with a smile.

I gave a playful smile and sighed.

"The question," I began, "was, will you marry me?" I told him.

"I will," he responded with a huge smile on his face.

I laughed.

"No! You are supposed to ask me that question!" I protested to him.

"I don't understand, Wynne. You just proposed, I accepted, so now why do I have to ask you?" he said to me as he took another bite of our sundae.

"Richard Carradine, don't you play games with me!" I said to him.

"Oh, honey, I'm not playing games! You proposed, I accepted, and now our sundae is melting. Hurry up and eat your part before it's all gone." He said to me as he plunged his spoon back into the ice cream.

Feeling somewhat flustered, I did as he suggested, not thinking twice about it. I made sure I dug to the bottom where the gooey hot fudge had melted. Bringing the spoon to my mouth, I look a bite and bit into something hard.

Pulling the spoon from my mouth, I looked down and saw something round and shiny amongst the spoonful of ice cream that was still left on the spoon.

"Rich, what is this?" I asked him as a huge smile lit his face.

"Well, that, my dear, looks to me like it's a ring to go along with your proposal," he said to me in a teasing voice.

"Ah, but is the ring for me or for you?" I asked him with a smile.

"We'll just have to see, now won't we?" was his response as he took the ring off of the spoon and wiped it off with a napkin.

There in the napkin was a beautiful gold ring holding the largest solitary diamond I have ever seen.

Getting down on his knees, Richard took my hand and slowly placed the ring on my finger.

"Wynne, will you fulfill my lifelong dream of becoming your husband? Will you fill that place in my heart completely that belongs to you? Will you become my wife?" Richard asked me with love shining in his eyes.

I leaned down and kissed him. It was a kiss full of love and happiness, promises and dreams come true!

"I love you, Richard Carradine, and would love to spend the rest of my life making all your dreams come true," I answered him with a smile.

Who said dreams never come true?

The End

Printed in the United States
43571LVS00002B/31-132